The Girl Who Rode Into a Storm

(Detective work was never
so pleasurable or deadly)

By

J. Wayne Frye

An Old Tale of Mystery
With a Modern Twist

This book is written in Canadian English

TO: Benjamin Fisher

We shared a grand friendship in our youth when we were both just starting our careers. He starred in my cult classic one-word movie, *Simba*. He never became a big Hollywood star, but he will always be the star of a New Jersey cult classic!

And

To: Jerry Paul

Sometimes we have no idea how a few acts of random kindness can endear you to someone. Long ago, in high school, I showed kindness to Jerry, and to his credit, he never forgot me.

Also, as always to my muse:

Lynton Globa Viñas – the dynamic dynamo.

Catalogue Number: 971381-2017

ISBN: 978-1-928183-33-4

Fireside Books – Canadian Division
Part of the Peninsula Publishing Consortium

THE GIRL WHO RODE INTO A STORM

Table of Contents

THE GIRL WHO RODE INTO A STORM

ABOUT THE AUTHOR

Wayne Frye's *Aaron Adams* mysteries, *Chablis Louise Chavez* thrillers, *Girl* books and *Lynton* adventures titillate the brains of those who enjoy tantalizing tales. His life, like the heroes he writes about, has been filled with adventure and excitement.

He has been a college hockey coach, professor, and at one time, the youngest university president in the USA. Called a marketing genius by the *Los Angeles Times*, he has been a promotional consultant to hockey teams and motion picture companies. He has been cited for his social work with gangs in Los Angeles and is active in the anti-globalization movement. A proud Canadian, he divides his time between Ladysmith, British Columbia; Laguna, Philippines and Cape Town, South Africa. He provides satirical political commentary to many Canadian newspapers.

Some of the 44 books by J. Wayne Frye

White Meteors and the Ghost of Sue Ann McGee
Hockey Mania and the Mystery of Nancy Running Elk
Something Evil in the Darkness at Hopkins House
How Hockey Saved a Jew From the Holocaust
The Girl Who Stirred up the Whirlwind
The Girl Who Motivated Murder Most Foul
The Girl Who Said Goodbye for the Last Time
Sammy Sasquatch and the Sts'ailes Star
Fall From Apocalypse
Armageddon Now
Worth Part 1: Roaring Through Life Like a Comet in the Midnight Sky
Worth Part 2: The Night of Thunder Road
When Jesus Came to Jersey as the Son of Thunder
When Jesus Came to Canada to Lead an Indigenous Rebellion
Canadian Angels of Mercy – Nurses in Times of Peril
Points of Rebellion: Aboriginals Who Fought for Justice
Lynton Walks on Water
Lynton Curls Her Hair
Lynton and the Vampire at Tagaytay Manor
Lynton Buys a Cell-Phone and Hears the Voice of Doom
Lynton Viñas and Beowulf Perez in the Taal Inferno
Lynton and the Ghosts in the Mansion on Balete Drive
Lynton Viñas: Shadow in the Darkness
Lynton's South African Adventure
Lynton, the Karoo Vampire and the Jewels of Omar Bin Abi
Lynton and the Stellenbosch Terror
Chablis: Avenging Angel for the Forgotten
In the City of Lost Hope
Chablis and the Terrorist
Pursuit
The Disappearance

J. WAYNE FRYE

Prologue
Take a Stand for Justice

There are those who walk in the shadows of mystery, individuals who by their very presence on the stage of life make others imagine what it would be like to stride down a dusty street with an air of confidence born of determination and will-power unencumbered by the constraints of a society that demands conformity. There are few individuals with the intestinal fortitude to defy convention and make their way into history for a brief moment when their majestic grandeur of purpose is sanctified and glorified by those with less determination. Dudley Danforth was such a person, and although this is a tale about a brief time in Dudley's life, it is also a plea to those of us who fall short in mustering the courage to stand against those who force us into submissive obedience to the privileged and powerful who have exerted control in society since man evolved from sea creatures and scurried onto dry land.

And for those who do not believe in evolution, believe in this: There are always a few storm riders out there just waiting to bring a little justice to a world where it is in very short supply. Many beleaguered weary travelers in this thing called life believe in grand and glorious justice in the sweet by and by, as they humbly wait to walk those streets in heaven paved with gold while they are abused, defiled and enslaved by the 1% at the top of the economic ladder in the here and now. Dudley Danforth never believed in heaven, but did believe in a man-made hell that trapped most people on a merry-go-round where the brass ring was always dangled but was never really within reach. Even in 1893, Dudley saw the real America, a land where wealth and privilege accrued to the few at the expense of the many. Nothing has changed in all these years, as today the privileged few rule with absolute power while the rest of us languish in obscurity scrambling for crumbs from the table of plenty set for the exalted few. Therefore, this is not just Dudley's story, but the story of the possibility that within us all might lay that spark that will make us bind together in an assault on complacency and finally take a stand for justice.

Chapter 1
Come Hope and Embrace Me

Conner McCord came into the town as a solid, slowly moving dust cloud. The gallop of his horse played a sweet symphony of determination. He was not distinctly visible until, as he stopped in front of the hotel, he gracefully climbed out of the saddle onto the ground. It was evident that the animal was in the last stages of exhaustion, with pleading eyes, hanging head and forelegs braced widely apart, while the sweat dripped steadily from its flanks. Plainly the horse had been pushed to the last limit of its strength.

The rider, dressed in black, was almost as exhausted as his horse, but despite the exhaustion, he did not walk up the hotel steps, but swaggered up them. He was a man in his early 30's, wide-shouldered and stoic looking. He was thin, but not painfully so and there was a look, oh what a look. One could see immediately that this was not a man with whom one should trifle.

Thick layers of dust clung to his shirt. Dust, too, made a mask of his face, and through that mask the eyes peered out, surrounded by bronzed skin somewhat leathered by exposure to the sun. The long, solemn face could have been called handsome, but it was more likely to be described as rugged good looks. But, on this particular day, he seemed a haunted man.

The two men starting out the door of the hotel, without a word, instinctively stepped aside and made room for him to go in. There was fear in their eyes as they observed Conner. He had no desire to enter the building. Suddenly he became doubly imposing, as he stood on the hotel porch and stared up and down at the men.

"Gentlemen," he politely said, as he scratched behind his left ear, "is there anybody in this town can sell me a horse? I have pressing business in Dry Gulch in three hours time."

"Well, don't know nobody wants to sell a horse, but if 'un you can find one, they's a short cut over that there mountain," one man said as he pointed to the dust laden mountain in the distance. "It's a mighty hard ride, but it'll cut over an hour off 'un the trip to Dry Gulch."

"I'll take it then."

The other man shaking his head grimly said, "Not a good idea if you ain't rode it before. I used to go that way when I was a young man, but nowadays nobody rides that way except Dudley. That trail is mighty tricky; you'd sure get lost without a guide."

Conner turned and followed the gesture of the speaker. The mountain rose from the very verge of the town, a ragged mass of sand and rock, with miserable sagebrush clinging here and there, as dull and uninteresting as the dust itself. Disgusted, he said, "I guess it ain't my cup of tea then. But I got to get to Dry Gulch in three hours."

"They's one hoss in town can get you there," one man said. "But I know it ain't gonna be available."

Conner sighed long and deep. "Then I'll make another one do."

"Can't be done. Dudley's horse is the only one could do it that quick, for sure. You'd kill another horse trying to make it that fast, even without going over the mountain."

Conner, dejected, asked, "But why can't I get that horse?"

"Dudley ain't around right now."

"I gotta get to Dry Gulch right away. It's life or death to me – life or death. Where's Dudley's horse?"

"Right across the road," said the older of the two men. "Yonder in the corral."

Conner turned and looked across at the corral and gazed upon a sleek looking magnificent steed. At that moment the horse raised its head and whinnied, looking straight at Conner, and their eyes locked on one another. Conner saw victory in that creature, victory against time. He made long, rapid strides in the mare's direction, but the two men came hurriedly after him, and the oldest fellow, grabbing his right arm said, "You ain't gonna take the horse without Dudley's permission is you?"

"Gentlemen, I gotta," said a dismayed Conner. "Listen! My name's Conner McCord. Up in my country they know I'm straight-up and honest; here you ain't heard of me. I ain't going to keep the horse, and I'll pay a hundred dollars for the use of her for a day. I'll bring or send her back, tomorrow. Here's the money. One of you gentlemen give it to him."

Neither man reached out; each head shook vehemently in the negative. "I'm too fond of the little life that's left to me," said the old fellow. "I won't take your money even if you give me a hundred dollars to take it. Why he loves that there mare like she was his wife. I'm a telling you that horse is like gold to him."

"No," the other man said, "Ain't no man treats his wife as good as Dudley treats that there horse. He loves it more than his own self I tell ya. He'd kill any man who tried to take that horse – flat out kill him."

But Conner McCord needed that horse. He had lost all reason as he saw that horse as his salvation while precious time ticked away. He knew, as well as he knew anything, that, once in the saddle on her, he would be sure to get to Dry Gulch in less than three hours. Nothing could stop him now, because his mind was made up.

The older man, with a tone of deep seriousness, pleaded with him. "Mister, don't be a fool. Maybe you don't recognize the name of Dudley, but don't let the name fool you. His nickname is Deadly Dudley Danforth.

Into the back of Conner's mind came several faint memories, but they were obscure and uncertain. "I don't care what his name is," he replied. "I gotta have that horse, and, if none of you'll take money for it, I'll take her free and pay her rent when I come through this way tomorrow. So long."

He went back across the street and undid the cinches of his own horse. He pulled the dusty old saddle and bridle off quickly, shouted to the hotel keeper, who had come to the door and was observing all the commotion, instructions to care for the weary animal and he'd pay when he returned. He ran across the road with the saddle on his arm.

In the corral he had no difficulty with the mare. She came straight to him in spite of all the flopping trappings. With prickly ears and eyes lighted with kindly curiosity she looked the dusty fellow over, as if sizing him up for worthiness to mount up.

He slipped the bridle over her head. When he swung the saddle over her back she merely turned her head and carelessly watched it fall. And when he drew up the cinches hard, she whined a bit. He mounted up and there was no resistance from the horse.

He looked across the street to the porch of the hotel, as he passed through the gate of the corral. The men were standing beside one another with looks of concern; their eyes wide and their mouths agape in awe at what was taking place. Whoever Dudley Danforth was, he was certainly a man who commanded fear if not respect, maybe both, thought Conner. The men on the porch looked at Conner as if he was a dead man astride a horse. He defiantly waved his hand at them and the mare, with one giddy-up from Conner, sprang into a determined gallop that started them rapidly down the street and out of the town.

The mare carried him with amazing speed over the dusty ground. They rounded the base of the big mountain, and, glancing up at the ragged terrain, which chopped the face of the peak, he was glad that he had not attempted that short cut. If Dudley could make that trail, he was an incredible horseman Conner thought as he kept reflecting back on the name Deadly Dudley Danforth.

Conner's route hugged the left shoulder of the mountain and he found himself looking down on the wide plain where he saw Dry Gulch in the far distance. The air was crystal-clear and dry, but the dust made him cough to clear his throat. Far away across the plain he saw a tiny moving dot that grew slowly. It was the train heading for Dry Gulch, and it was the train that he had to beat to the station. For a moment his heart stood still; then he saw that the train was distant indeed, and, by the slightest use of the mare's speed, he would be able to reach the town five or ten minutes ahead of it. He urged the horse on with haste. The heart of Conner skipped a beat, and he went cold with doubt. It was not only the fear that his journey might be ruined, but the fear that something had happened to this magnificent creature beneath him. He swung to the side in the saddle and watched her gallop slower, labouring, very much as though she were trying to run against a mighty pull on the reins.

He looked at her head. It was thrown high, with pricking ears. Perhaps she was frightened by some foolish thing near the road. He reluctantly touched her with the spurs, and she increased her pace to the old length and ease of stride; but, just as he had begun to be reassured, her step shortened and fell to labouring again, and this time she threw her head higher than before. Then it seemed to Conner that he heard a faint, far whistling sound floating down from high above his head.

It was then that he looked up toward a small butte and saw a horseman furiously plunging down the side of the mountain. He knew instantly that it was Danforth. The man had come to confront the person he considered a thief.

Conner was not frightened, but he had no time to face-off against a man who was justifiably upset. He did not want to kill a man over a misunderstanding of intent, but he had no time to explain and no time to tarry. He figured that, although Dudley was slanting to his left in anticipation of intercepting him up the road, he would be a fraction short. By the time he came down onto the trail, the swift horse under Conner would be well ahead, and certainly no horse lived that was capable of overtaking Conner's swift mount. Never one to use his spurs, this time Conner gently flicked the horse with them, but she reared straight up and, whirling to the side, faced steadily toward her onrushing master.

Again and again Conner spurred the animal, feeling the pain himself, and lamenting his desperation to get the animal moving. She winced from the pain and snorted, but, apparently having not the slightest knowledge of bucking, she could only shake her head and send a ringing whinny of appeal up the slope of the mountain toward the approaching rider.

Despite the impending danger and untenable delay which was ruining his chances of getting to Dry Gulch before the train, Conner could not help but watch with awe at the sure and determined horsemanship of the man coming down the mountain.

Even as the mare under Conner stopped in answer to the signal of her owner, Danforth sent his mount over the edge of a nearly vertical cliff, pulling the horse back on its haunches, seeming to literally get airborne on the rock-laden slope, careening from side to side as a rush of pebbles flew about him and a dust cloud whirled into a frenzy. Conner just sat there astride the horse and knew his goal of reaching Dry Gulch before the train was now probably irreversibly impaired. His only alternative was to shoot Danforth, and he was not prepared to do that, or was he?

Danforth broke out onto the road ahead of Conner, and he pulled his horse's reins back making her whinny softly as Conner's own horse greeted her master with a nod of the head. Conner found himself looking into the surprisingly smooth face of as stern a man as he had ever seen, noticing he was a dashingly handsome fellow, several years younger than Conner, a high-headed, straight-eyed and buoyant type. In the poise of his demeanour and the play of his hand on the reins, Conner recognized a man of courage despite being of a very small size, maybe no more than 5:5. As Danforth halted his horse in the middle of the road and looked with deadly eyes at Conner, he appeared to be a giant of sternness, but there was a soft quality about the way he held the reins.

"You're Dudley, I guess," said Conner, "and you know that I've done you a wrong by taking this horse. But I wanted to pay for it, and I'll pay now. I've got to get to Dry Gulch before that train down there," he said as he pointed at the chugging train in the far distance. "I haven't hurt her any. Her wind isn't touched. She's pretty wet from sweat, but I never spurred her hard, only a light tap when I feared I would have to tangle with you, which I do not want to do."

Not cracking a smile, Danforth replied in a high pitched voice, "Better to run off with a man's wife than his best horse. A good wife isn't hard to find, but a good mount is mighty hard to come by."

"Mr. Danforth, I am desperate. I need to beat that train to Dry Gulch."

"Stealing a horse is inexcusable."

Conner was trying to control his desperation as he watched that train move closer and closer to Dry Gulch, while he was being way-laid by a man with no understanding and no concern for anything but his damn horse. Beyond him, the train was looming larger and larger on the plain, and Dry Gulch seemed more distant than ever.

"I tell you I'll pay. I'll pay whatever you want, and still return it to you."

Danforth rode over beside his horse and looked at its shanks. Again, Conner was taken aback by his high pitched voice. "I can see you were gentle with your spurs, but still no spur has ever touched that horse. Nope, no one ever dared spur that horse. No one, I tell you, no one."

"Look, I'm sorry."

"What part of the world you come from where they teach you to spur a fine animal like that?"

"I'll tell you after I get to Dry Gulch."

"I'll shoot you before I see you in Dry Gulch."

"Look, I am trying to be patient, but time is wasting, and I got urgent business in Dry Gulch."

Danforth smiled and said, "Well, I'd say you have more urgent business here, because horse thievery gets a man killed in these parts."

Ordinarily, Conner avoided a fight at all costs, but the time element and the interagency of

Danforth flared a sudden anger within him, rising to a level that brought an impulse to kill in order to get rid of this obstacle between him and everything he wanted most in life. Without warning, he reluctantly snatched out his pistol. Certainly all the approaches to a fight had been made, and Danforth had obviously been expecting the attack, because just as the gun ripped out of Conner's holster, Danforth swung himself sidewise in his own saddle, snapping his revolver, firing while the gun was still holstered.

That swerve to the side saved him from the shot fired by Conner; while Danforth's bullet ploughed cleanly through Conner's right thigh. He went numb from the pain, dropping his gun as he clung with both hands to lower himself out of the saddle. He collapsed in the dust of the trail and stared, not at Danforth, but at the train that was now pulling into Dry Gulch. He was defeated.

Danforth knelt beside him and examined the wound. "It's clean," he said, as he started ripping up the lower part of his shirt to make a bandage. "I'll have you fixed so you can get to a doctor."

He began to work rapidly, twisting the torn material around Conner's thigh, but all Conner could see now was the train pulling out of Dry Gulch after a brief stop. The sound of the belching engine filtered up the side of the ravine below.

Conner bowed his head, as the pain meant nothing to him. He had been shot much worse before. The real pain was in his aching heart. "I was a fool," he said.

Smiling, Danforth replied, "You won't get an argument from me there."

Smiling back, Conner emphatically apologized. "I am sincerely sorry I took that horse. It was irresponsible of me."

"Well," replied Danforth, "that horse is awfully special. It is the most valuable thing I have. When I saw you spur her that was the final straw. That there horse has seen me through some tough spots and never once did I spur her."

Conner was taken with the refinement illustrated by Danforth. He was obviously an educated man, and, although there was a rugged demeanour about him, one could sense a sophisticated and polished nature. Obviously, he was not prone to hard work with his hands, as they were not calloused or hard. They actually felt soft and warm as the bandage was wrapped around the wound. He had a gentle, caring touch.

"Truth is Mr. Danforth that is the very first time in my life that I ever spurred a horse," offered Conner.

"I believe you. Name is Dudley by the way."

"I am mighty sorry I drew down on you Dudley. It was the act of desperation by a mighty foolish man."

Shaking his head left to right, Dudley said, "Well, maybe we both reacted a bit hastily, but I assumed you for a horse thief and maybe a gunfighter too. I was a bit crazed I guess. That horse is the best friend I have. I am really sorry this happened. Maybe you could tell me why you risked being accused of horse thievery to get to that town down there so all-fired quick."

"I was going to Dry Gulch to meet a girl."

"Must be some kind of special girl to warrant what you went through. And I messed it up. But why didn't you tell me what you wanted?"

"I just didn't have any chance. Besides I could not waste time talking and explaining to anybody."

"Sure you couldn't, but the girl will forgive you when she finds out what happened."

"No, she won't, because she'll never find out."

"What do you mean by that?" replied Dudley.

"I don't know where she will be. It's a long story, and I'm about to pass out."

Dudley sighed with a look of deep concern on his face and said, as he pulled Conner under a tall scrub bush on the side of the road, "You rest here out of the sun and I'll go into Dry Gulch and get a buckboard. You are in no shape for riding a horse. I'll be back in 30 or 40 minutes."

"I'm much obliged to you."

Thirty minutes later the buckboard arrived and the wounded man was helped on to a pile of blankets in the back of the wagon. The shooting, of course, was explained as nothing but a gun accident. As they told it, Dudley happened to be passing along the same route and saw Conner looking over his revolver as he rode along. At that moment the gun went off and hit him in the leg. The tale was accepted, but no one believed it, as the people in Dry Gulch knew Dudley's reputation and also were familiar with the two horses, both of which were obviously his. Still, if that is what these two men wanted people to believe, the townspeople and the sheriff saw no reason to pry any further.

The trip in was a painful one for Conner, not only as a result of the wound but because of exhaustion from the three days trip in pursuit of the girl who was on that train. The pain in the leg was secondary to the pain in his heart from the sense of frustrated failure and loss. Never in his life had he fought so bitterly and steadily for a thing, and yet he had lost it at the very verge of success. Despondency overwhelmed this usually strong man with an iron will.

In the meantime, the people of Dry Gulch were delighted to have Dudley in town. Beyond all others, this was a man who had one of those personalities that though he was to be feared, there was something about him that had to be described as magically, lyrically, incredibly, wondrously dynamic.

Whatever Dudley did, it seemed greater because he was the one who did it. He gave everyone around the feeling that this was a man capable of great and astonishing things. Men older than he were willing to accept him as their leader; men younger than he idolized him.

He leaned in the doorway of the Dry Gulch Hotel and Emporium, looking out at the street while people congregated around him. He was wearing a too big denim shirt with a red bandana tied around his neck. It was loosely knotted and the ends were separated, one hanging to the front and one to the back. His hat was perhaps an actual work of art the way he wore it. It was black with a wide brim and the right front of it was creased down, but on him it was more than just a hat. It added a devil-may-care attitude to a man who spoke of distinction as a rugged individualist. This was a man who did not have to ask for respect. It was given, and something else was also evident if you dared mess with him. This was a man to be feared, but still there was gentleness to him that everyone could sense. He never used profanity, did not smoke nor drink, and despite being the object of great attention from the women, he seemed uninterested.

He, for some reason, had not removed his riding gloves, and for a man approaching 30, he actually did not even have a hint of a beard. The gloves suited a horseman, but not a range-roving cowboy, as Dudley could not handle a rope, nor could he tell the noose end of a lariat from the straight end. Neither did he know the slightest thing about barbed wire at a time when it was being used to fence off areas in a nation where the free range was being gobbled up by barons of greed who wanted to own more and more, while fencing off all their holdings. It was as if the whole country was becoming obsessed with placing labels of ownership on everything from the medicine in the drug stores to the water that had flowed so freely through the wilderness until it was damned up and fenced off by the cattle barons. And through it all, the government always stood with the rich and privileged over the poor and unprivileged. But Dudley was an independent soul who never bowed before any man or any government.

Dudley slowly removed his gloves and placed them in his back left pocket. His hands were small, and frankly, for a tough man, a bit feminine looking. His fingers were long, slender and bony. The wrists were round and dainty looking, almost as innocent of sinews as the wrists of a woman, but, most remarkable of all, the skin of the palms of those hands was amazingly soft, as if he was a cowboy who simply did not cotton to the more commonplace duties of a ranch hand.

There were some who shook their heads when they saw those hands. There were a few who inferred that Dudley was little better than a prancer of swagger, and that, in reality, he had never done a better or more useful thing than handle cards and a revolver. In both of which arts it was admitted that he was incredibly dexterous. As a matter of fact, since there was no known source from which he drew an income, and since he had never been known in the entire history of his young life to do a single stroke of productive hard work, the truth was that outside an occasional horse trading that he derived most of his income from gambling. Yet, within his thin frame beat a kinder heart than most gambler's possessed as he hated taking money from less clever gamblers when they were intoxicated, and he also lacked the fine hardness of mind which enables many gamblers to enjoy taking the last cent from an opponent. Also, although he knew the entire retinue of tricks in the repertoire of a crooked gambler, he had never been known to employ those tricks, instead, replying on his generally superior skills. He trusted in a calm head, a quick judgment and an ability to read an opponent's facial expressions to intricately decipher whether he was holding a solid hand or was bluffing. Few were his equal at the card table, except maybe a woman who played on occasion in town. Her name was Deanna Defoe, but she and Dudley had never met at the card table or even in any other forum, as it seemed they were always just missing each other somehow, but everyone often wondered what it would be like to observe the two of them in card combat on the battlefield of poker. Although both had occasionally played against crooked professionals who were wolves in the guise of sheep, no one had ever been known to play more than one crooked trick at cards when coming up against either one.

Dudley and Deanna alike made a good living at the card table, and both had stared down crooks with careful aplomb, and both knew how to use a gun. Dudley with a Colt 45 strapped to his hip, and Deanna with a deadly two shot derringer under the sleeve of her blouse that she had hooked up to a slide mechanism, making it flick out faster than lighting. On occasion, Deanna, similar to Dudley, would even strap two 45's around her thin waist, making her dainty, silk dresses accentuate a figure that turned many a man's head, but kept them at a distance out of fear she might react adversely to any romantic advances. She also would strap a gun to her left thigh on occasion.

As Dudley removed his gloves that day, all around him were sure that delicate right hand had pulled the trigger that felled the stranger in town, but none dared be accusatory. His hands were his stock and trade and what lovely hands they were, often displaying wiggling fingers dancing with the desire to play cards and feel those coated lasses of money mayhem with the tips of his fingers, so that they seemed to be of independent intelligence.

He crossed his unusually small feet. His boots were the finest leather, bench-made by the best of boot makers, and they fitted the high-arched instep with elastic smoothness, and the heels were extra high. So high that he had an almost womanly rhythmic sway to his hips with each stride he took, but none there dared ever mention, even to a friend, that he exhibited feminine qualities in the way he walked.

Those boots were his pride and joy. They were rubbed and polished to softness and brightness before this luxurious dressed gambler would walk about town. From the heels of the boots extended a long pair of spurs, surely a very great vanity, for he would never allow the touch of a spur on any horse he was astride. The spurs were more a design accessory than a necessity. They were plated with a touch of gold, and they swept up and out in a long, exquisite curve, the hub of the rowel set with fake diamonds. Yep, Dudley was more than just a tough man, he was a fashion statement!

Oh, and his immensely long, dense, dark hair dangled way down his back in a pony tail and when he walked, it fluttered gorgeously below his wide brimmed hat, as if fluffed by an invisible hand. Yes, Dudley Danforth was a dandy among men, with a peculiarity that he seemed to dress to please himself more than the rest of the world. His glances never roved about taking account of the admiration of others, but one could sense that he did enjoy the attention garnered. As he leaned there in the doorway of the hotel, he was the type of young, happy, genuine and carefree fellow whose mind is no heavier with a thousand dollars or a dollar in his pocket. He was attuned to the glory of life, but still, there was something strange, something that was hollow within his magnificent frame. There was a secret Dudley hid, a secret that was somehow kept in the dark recesses of a mind that longed to let out the truth, a truth that might well make him a pariah among his peers. He had kept the secret for a long time now, and it was something that preyed upon his psyche, sometimes driving him to near total desperation, but always he managed to control it, but only up to a point, then like a meandering, calm river flowing gracefully and peacefully toward a raging water fall, he could no longer restrain himself and had to embrace the truth, the naked truth of his inner mind, inner self, inner turmoil that had to roar over the precipice and plunge downward into a calm pool where the clean, pure water of hope flowed gracefully.

Suddenly he started from his lounging place, cocked his hat just a bit more than usual and hurried across the veranda of the hotel. Had he seen an enemy to chastise, or an old friend to greet? No, it was only old Jess Hanley, the blacksmith. He was staggering under a load of boards which he had shouldered to carry to his shop. In a moment, part of that load was shifted to Dudley's shoulder and they went on down the street, laughing and talking together until the load was dropped on the floor of Hanley's shop.

"And how's that fellow you brought in to town doing?" asked Hanley.

"He'll be fine in a couple of days. Lucky thing it was a clean wound and didn't nick the bone. Soon as it's healed over he'll never know he was shot."

"Queer thing to me," Hanley said, "is how you and this fellow have hit it off so well together. Might almost say it was like you'd shot him and now was trying to make up for it. But, of course, that ain't the case."

"Of course not," replied Dudley.

"Another queer thing," offered Hanley. "He was fooling with that gun while he was on the horse, which just means that the muzzle must of been pretty close to his skin. But there wasn't any sign of a powder burn, the doc says."

"What? You some kind of blooming detective now, Jess?"

THE GIRL WHO RODE INTO A STORM

He shrugged his shoulders and got a serious look on his face. "I got something to tell you, Dudley. Ever hear the story about the gent that took pity on the snake that was stiff with cold and brought the snake in to warm him up beside the fire? The minute the snake come to life it sunk its fangs in the gent that had saved him."

"Meaning," said Dudley, "that, because I've done a good turn for a guy, I'd still better look out for him?"

"Meaning nothing," said Hanley, "except that the reason the snake bit the gent was because he'd had a stone heaved at him by the same man one day and hadn't forgot it."

"You know what Jess, maybe instead of a blacksmith you should have been a philosopher."

"Ain't no money in philosophizing."

Dudley grinned, waved goodbye and headed across the street. He sighed and thought of Conner, and how he had maybe contributed to messing up his chance at happiness. He didn't know the whole story, but thought that the woman he was in a hurry to meet must be a real beauty. Conner was a good looking guy and would no doubt have a good looking girlfriend, but why had he risked so much in pursuit of her? Still, he was foolish to take a horse without asking.

That you are fair or wise is vain,
Or strong, or rich, or generous;
You must have also the untaught strain
That sheds beauty on the rose.
There is a melody born of melody,

THE GIRL WHO RODE INTO A STORM

Which melts the world into a sea:
Toil could never compass it;
Art its height could never hit;
It came never out of wit.
There is something within Dudley
That is a growing raging fire,
Which drives a sweet low desire.
What within his spirits will lift
His eternal search for a special gift?
Alas! That one is born in blight,
Victim of a perpetual slight.
He is blind but will eventually see.
Come hope and embrace me!

J. WAYNE FRYE

Chapter 2
Find the Woman He Loved

Conner McCord had been a strange patient. He had never repeated his offer to tell his story. He remained sullen and silent, with his brooding eyes fixed on the ceiling above him, and nothing could permanently cheer him up. Some inward gloom seemed to possess him, to have taken hold on his psyche and rendered him in a state of perpetual melancholy, almost as if he was hiding a truth that might put him in an untenable position.

The first day after the shooting he had insisted on penning a painfully written letter, while Dudley propped a writing board in front of him, as he lay half-sitting in the bed, but that was his only act indicating any real interest in life, and it was an act that appeared to drain him more emotionally than physically. No one saw the letter, as it was sealed immediately and handed to a lawyer who had been called in by Conner to see that it got to the address on the envelope, an address that the lawyer was duty bound not to reveal under strict attorney-client privilege. Thereafter, Conner remained mostly silent and brooding. Perhaps it was hatred for Dudley who had laid him low that was growing in him, as the sense of disappointment increased, for Dudley, after all, had kept him from reaching that girl when the train had briefly passed through town.

Perhaps, for all Dudley knew, his bullet had ruined the happiness of two people. He entertained that disagreeable thought, and, reaching the hotel, he went straight up to his room and lay down on the bed, drifting off into what would be a three day disappearance where he just lounged in his room while Conner was removed from the small backroom clinic at the doctors and placed in a room down the hall from Dudley.

Being ignored by Dudley actually bothered Conner, but his concern was alleviated a bit when he heard from the maid that a beautiful woman named Deanna Defoe had arrived in town and was downstairs playing poker. She told Conner she would have someone come up and help move him down to the saloon area of the hotel, so he could watch this marvel play poker.

Two men from the saloon came up and helped Conner downstairs, where he was placed at a table across from the six people, among them Deanna

Defoe, who were playing poker. He was given a pillow to sit on, and another one to rest his back upon. Never had Conner McCord seen such a radiantly beautiful woman than Deanna Defoe. He even sensed the beautiful woman who had been on that train could not compare to Deanna Defoe, who was, without a doubt, the most fascinatingly magnificent, resplendent, effulgent and mysterious looking creature of the female species that he had ever had the privilege to gaze upon. There was just something unreal and eerie about her, something almost recognizable in her mannerisms but he could not get his mind to connect the pieces of the growing puzzle. Her face, incredibly luminous, had a glowing radiance. The eyes were a piercingly sharp shade of brown. Eyebrows were arched high and mildly thick, and lined with mascara that made her appear exotic and mysterious. A tiny, dainty nose set off two rosy, slightly plump cheeks on each side that seemed to be just lightly sprinkled with the stardust of an angel come to earth, but you knew this was a deadly angel who tolerated no alienation of affections from men who were eager to bed this damsel of delight. Plump, succulent lips had the sensual curl to them that made Conner tingle when he thought about how delightful it would be to plant a kiss on them and taste the sweetness in their moisture. Her enchanting face was framed by wavy, dark red-coloured curls, falling gracefully to her shoulders seeming to lure the hands of a man to gently caress their softness.

THE GIRL WHO RODE INTO A STORM

She seemed like a queen, high and regal, with a strange air of mystery that was as titillating as her beauty. Conner could tell she was sensing his gaze, although she never looked his way. He scanned downward around her tight bodice that hugged a heavenly figure, slender but somewhat muscular for a woman. She did not reflect an overtly feminine body like a porcelain ornament and seemingly fragile, as although she looked to be light as a feather, one could sense there was a lethalness to her, and that anyone who dared mess with her might well pay a heavy price. Her body seemed so agile looking that one could imagine her gliding as she moved swiftly across a meadow, the hem of her dress sweeping the grass wet with dew as though she were floating slightly above the ground. Her eyes held a distant, dreamy look within them, yet seemed to scan her opponents with purpose and intent. Whenever her eyes met those of an opponent they held within them an eerily knowing look as though she could see right into their minds and knew exactly what cards they were holding.

The betting went around the table, each man tossing the necessary chips down to call until it got to her, the dealer for the hand. She smiled, tossed in the same amount to stay in the game, and then a more knowing smile creased her lips as she said in a low, husky, soft, peacefully soothing voice, "And I raise $100."

All, but one man folded. He sat staring at her, contemplating what to do. He said, "I fold."

THE GIRL WHO RODE INTO A STORM

She appeared pleased as she tossed her cards on the table. The man to her left started to turn them over, but she placed her hand on his and said, "You didn't pay to see those cards."

"But I did pay. I had over $50 in that pot and folded."

"You didn't call me mister. It costs another $100 to see my cards," she said as she picked up her cards, then picked up the discards and skilfully mixed hers in with them.

The man was seething with anger now, saying nothing, but you could see he was thinking about reaching for his gun. Deanna looked him straight in the eyes as she said, "You won't clear your holster with that gun before I put a bullet between your eyes. Be very careful with your next move. It could be your last."

The man beside him placed his left hand on the man's right hand and said, "Let it go Everett. This is not a woman you want to mess with."

Everett pushed his chair back so hard and so fast that it tumbled over onto the floor. He stormed out in a huff, never looking back. Deanna looked at the man who had saved Everett's life and said, "Thanks Shane, I'd hate to end my day with a killing."

Straightening herself up, she looked over at Conner and gave him a slow, methodical smile that crept across those succulent, ruby red lips penetrating into his soul, boring deep into his psyche and rattling his brain with thoughts of what an extraordinary woman this was.

THE GIRL WHO RODE INTO A STORM

She finished her drink, which was apple juice, and rose to her feet like a lioness that had just made a kill. Gangly as a willow, but shapely in all the right places, she reached for her cloak on the back of her chair and threw it about her somewhat broad shoulders, slowly bringing her surprisingly small but perky little breasts into sharp pointed and erect mode as the nipples seemed to be pointing directly at Conner. She smiled at him again, and he felt ashamed that he was letting another woman filter into a mind that had just missed the opportunity of a lifetime with that girl on the train.

He glanced around the room and was amused to see how many eyes were now fixed on Deanna. You could tell she enjoyed the effect she had on men. She played her womanliness just as effectively as she played her cards.

She looked over at Shane and said, as she pushed her pile of chips toward him. "Cash me in. I'll be around later to pick up my winnings and buy you a drink or two."

"Make it three," said a laughing Shane.

"You got it, big boy," Deanna replied.

All conversation stopped as she gracefully glided from the room and there was universal joy felt by all present as evidenced in the deep sighs of amazement and the relaxation of more than one set of shoulders among the men who were simply made into snivelling, worshipful idiots in her presence, and how she enjoyed it. On the way out, she looked down at Conner and gave him a wink.

THE GIRL WHO RODE INTO A STORM

Watching her saunter out the swinging doors in her high heels made her swaying hips seem to play a rousing symphony with kettle drums banging a rhythm of erotic delight. Conner watched the doors swing shut, and he suddenly felt that a Rembrandt of eroticism had just had a black drape placed over it. He looked around the room, crowded with men and a few bar girls, and every one of them was still staring at those swinging doors, as if they were hoping, praying, begging for her to walk back in and brighten the drudgery with her glorious glamour that was like the bright sun rising from below the horizon each morning to bring warmth to a cold day.

For two more days, Conner kept having someone help him back down to the hotel saloon, and he watched with glee as Deanna played her graceful game of poker. He could never muster the courage to speak to her, and she never did anything more than smile at him on her way out each day. Then, just like the snapping of a finger, she was gone. Apparently, according to Shane, just scurrying out of town apparently in the dark, having left an envelope with the bar tender filled with payment on her tab and generous tips for the waitresses and even something for Shane, who had made sure she was well taken care of.

On the day of her departure, Dudley came down to the saloon and greeted Conner. "Sorry, I have been out of sorts lately," he said, looking down at Conner who was in the chair that had become his portal for observing Deanna.

"No problem," replied Conner. "I have been observing a very fascinating woman."

"Ah, no doubt you speak of the lovely Deanna Defoe. Few men can resist her charms. Never met her, but would like to do so some day."

"It will be a treat when you do. I cannot say when I have seen a finer lady in absolutely every way."

"It is nice to know that maybe you have not been spending all your time hating me. You still look a bit glum. No doubt, you are still blaming me for all the things that have happened to you."

The dark flush and the uneasy flicker of Conner's glance gave a sufficient answer to the question posed. He did, indeed, blame Dudley for his dilemma.

Dudley sighed and shook his head. "You don't have to talk. I see that I'm right. And I don't blame you, because, maybe through my overt inability to comprehend your true intentions, I over reacted. I am sorry, believe me."

At first, Conner's silence was almost an admission that he felt the same way about the matter, yet he finally said aloud, "I don't blame you. Maybe you thought I was a horse thief, because of the way I handled the matter. But the thing is done, and it won't ever be undone!"

Dudley pulled his seat up a little closer, and leaned in close enough for Conner to smell his breath. He had eaten something sweet as it had a pleasant smell that penetrated Conner's nostrils and made him wonder what he had eaten.

"Conner," said Dudley, "Do you know what you're going to do now?"

"Haven't really thought about it."

"You are going to tell me the whole story about you and that girl on the train you missed. You are not through with this little chase. Not if I have to drag you along with me. But first, just figure that I am not going anywhere nor are you until the whole truth is laid before me. Besides, it will help you considerably to unburden yourself to someone who really cares. If you feel like cussing me real good when the time comes, go ahead and cuss, but I think I really should hear the story."

"Maybe it would help," said Conner, "but it's a pretty sorry story to tell."

"Sorry or not, tell it to me. I'll be the judge."

Conner shifted himself to a more comfortable position, and as his mind was flooded with recollections, he noticed that Dudley was arching his eyebrows and that there was genuine interest in his eyes that were flashing a look that was, for some reason, recognizable. Conner had seen that look before. It was a look that spoke of compassion. Dudley was genuinely sorry for what had occurred, and he was trying to make it right. Thus began the tale: "It all started about maybe a year ago. I was up to the Severn Mountains working a gold claim that I had very carefully staked out. There wasn't much to it, just enough to keep me going for awhile, keep food on my table and offer me a chance to fix-up my cabin a bit. I pegged away at it pretty steady, leading a lonely life and hoping that I'd cut my way down to a good vein of gold one day. Well, the vein just wasn't there. It never showed up. Meantime, I got pretty weary of the old place and being all alone. I didn't even have a dog with me to at least talk at, so I got to thinking how I was wasting my life away, always looking for that pot at the end of the rainbow and never finding it. I just doubted so many things, every thing that is. Where was my life going I kept asking myself? What in my nearly 35 years had I ever accomplished? I'd never known the love of a woman, just rented one now and then for a few minutes at the time. There was never a connection with any of them, just a business arrangement that when it was over, I was shown the door. I was just sinking really low over my life in general."

Dudley interrupted with his soft, high-pitched voice seeming to quiver just a bit as he said, "I have been there in a way, my friend. I know the feeling of going to bed in my own place alone and wondering why I cannot find someone to share my hopes, dreams and aspirations. But I am sorry I interrupted you. Go on, please."

Nodding his head, Conner continued. "I started doubting things, doubting my whole life." Here he cast an envious glance at the smooth brow of his companion and continued. "I appreciate the fact you have had your own doubts, but I think you are just trying to make me feel good. The two most confident people I have seen of late are you and that woman, Deanna Defoe."

THE GIRL WHO RODE INTO A STORM

Smiling knowingly, Dudley got a mysterious look on his face and said, "Well, I have heard of Deanna Defoe, and no doubt she is a fine woman, but my guess is even she has her doubts. She puts up a good front, but, like I just admitted to you, I am sure, if she was honest, she would probably admit to a few doubts along the route she has taken in life."

"Well," went on Conner, "I got so tired of my own thoughts and of myself that I decided something had to be done; something to give me new things to think about. So I sat down and began to really take stock of my life. I had heard of these here correspondence schools that could teach you almost anything. I couldn't think of anything special I wanted to learn, but I knew that I wanted to learn something, wanted to stop just being an old unread, dumb cowboy. I picked me out one of them schools. It was called ICS, and it was actually right over in Minnesota. I wrote them a long letter telling them about my life, and how I wanted to become more learned. I didn't care what I studied. I just wanted to study. It didn't even have to be useful, just something that might elevate my intelligence a bit. Well, within two weeks, I got an answer back. What you think the school said?"

"I have no idea my friend. What?"

"Well, sir, the first thing they wrote back was: 'We have your letter and think that in the first place you had better learn how to write.' That was a pretty nasty answer, wasn't it?"

THE GIRL WHO RODE INTO A STORM

Through a half smile, Dudley replied, "Yes, not a good way to treat a potential customer."

"Every time I looked at that letter it sure made me mad. And I looked at it a hundred times a day and come near tearing it up every time. But I didn't, because I knew it was a woman who wrote it and that infuriated me even more that a woman would say those things. And you know it was the prettiest, most dainty handwriting I had ever seen. Her signature, Danielle Donnelly, was beautiful to just look at, like a work of art. There was a raw femininity to it, carefulness to each letter that seemed to just have so much womanliness in every single stroke of the pen. I could tell it was written with an old fashioned quill pen, and I began to think that each letter was her way, as, no doubt, a well-educated and well-bred woman, of telling me just how ignorant and backward I was. I mean she might have been a fine person, but she had no right to ridicule my ignorance."

"Definitely not," interjected Dudley. "But do not judge her too abruptly. Maybe she was just having a bad day when she wrote back. I mean people do things and do regret them, do realize they have handled a matter indelicately."

Getting a serious look on his face, Conner said, "Wait, I ain't through yet."

"Sorry, go on, please."

"Well, that letter made me so plumb mad that I sat down and wrote everything I could think of that a gent would say to a girl to let her know what I thought about her. I mean I let her have it from

J. WAYNE FRYE

both barrels, so to speak. And what do you think happened?"

"She wrote you back an apology, and said she was rude and inconsiderate. Asked you to forgive her, I bet."

Nodding his head affirmatively, Conner said, "Yep, you got that right. I mean she actually wrote it in such a way that I could almost feel her regret, her sorrowfulness of purpose; because she explained she just wanted to motivate me to learn to write better. Her response the second time was smooth as silk with every word seeming to be filled with honest regret. I mean I could almost sense that she was crying as she wrote the letter, but at the same time, there was a sense that she was sorry, but not for telling me what I needed, but in the way she wrote it. Just like you said, she explained she had a really bad day and was dealing with many personal problems that were preying heavily on her mind. So heavily that she let them interfere with her usual kindly, gentle, polite nature. She even said that she was a woman who was self-reliant; prideful of her looks and her education, and that she had let those things far too often make her too arrogant. Now, the first letter she signed with only her name, but this time, she added, Secretary to the President. But all she wrote down this time at the end of the letter was Regretfully Yours. Anyway that's the thing she done, right enough. She writes me a letter of apology and then puts a P.S. suggesting that I enrol in a composition course to learn how to write, saying she would personally oversee my studies to make sure I got what I needed."

"Sometimes Conner, first impressions are wrong. Sounds like this might be a lady who really has her act together, a woman who might be prideful of her looks, but not to the point of it interfering with her kindness, her commitment to treating all people with respect. I am sometimes too quick to act without thinking, myself, and I often regret it. I know people fear me, because I will not take any disrespect, but you ask around, and people will also tell you I am fair minded, and willing to admit a mistake. I am admitting to you that I got your intentions wrong, and I regret it, just like that woman did. She and I are similar it sounds like. But, I interrupted your story. Go on please."

"Well, Dudley, I am not one to carry a grudge, not one who doesn't have the ability to forgive. I thought it wouldn't do me no harm to unlimber my pen and fire out a few words to her. So I done it. I started writing her every day. She and I started writing back and forth and she told me to write about the things that was around me, and each time I wrote, she would respond just like a teacher with a lot of lessons about how you can't use the same word twice in the same sentence, and how terrible bad it is to use too many passive verbs. I mean the letters went back and forth like a whirlwind between us, and I am no scholar, but I felt like I was really learning from her. Then she starts asking me about where I live and asks me to describe the place. She actually gets really enthralled it seems and wants to see my place."

Dudley got a big smile on his face, as he said, "Then she began asking about you didn't she? She became interested in you. She was becoming impressed with you as a person of quality, a real gentleman."

"Confound you," said Conner. "How come you figured that out?"

"Well, it is pretty obvious you are a nice fellow, Conner. I should have taken more time to figure that out, but I made the same mistake as the little missy did. I reacted too fast without slow, methodical thought. I need to work on jumping to conclusions before thinking things through."

Conner, realizing he had made a good friend in Dudley, said, "Well, you know she never even sent me a picture all those months we were corresponding, but I knew she was a beautiful woman. Sometimes you can just tell. I did ask her for a picture, and she kept saying that I might be disappointed, but I knew the real reason she was not sending one was because she was a beautiful woman, and she had probably had too many men who went crazy over her looks without getting to know the real woman, the woman inside that was even more beautiful than the exterior. I stopped caring about a picture. I saw the real beauty of the woman in what she wrote. You know I envy writers, because they can use words to describe feelings, but I could never find words to describe how much I had fallen in love with her, sight unseen. I tell you Dudley, this is a woman like no other, and still she never revealed too much."

With a knowing look, Dudley said, "But you sent her a photo of you, because you wanted her to know what you looked like, to know what she might be getting."

"Who's telling this story, Dudley? You sure you don't know this girl. I mean Minneapolis is only a few hours' ride from where you live. Maybe you took some courses from that school. You seem like a mighty educated man."

"Nope, don't get to Minnesota but ever couple of years, but educated I am. Had a daddy who insisted I study at the Colorado School of Mines." Then he got a big smile and said, "Anyway, enough about me, what happened after you sent her a picture of that ugly mug of yours."

Laughing, Conner, replied, "Nothing, not a thing. Not a word came back from her to answer that letter I'd sent."

Well, if I was a woman, I'd probably give you a tumble, even with that ugly mug of yours. You got a rugged good looks to you, my friend. Maybe you didn't look rich enough to suit her tastes."

"I thought that, and I thought it was my ugly face that might have made her change her mind. I thought of pretty near everything else that was bad about me and that she might have read in my face. Sure made me sick for a long time. Somebody else was correcting my lessons. There was no letter from her, as the school must have bought one of those new fangled machines they call a typewriter, as all of a sudden all my lessons came back typewritten rather than written by hand."

"Well," interjected Dudley, "machines change everything, because you lose the personal touch. One day machines will run the world, and that will be a sorry day indeed, when the human touch is lost. Maybe she had good reasons for not writing; maybe something happened in her life that caused her to stop writing. Anyway, I know you didn't give up. You kept writing didn't you?"

"Nope, I didn't give up. I sat down and wrote a letter to the head of the school and told him I'd like to get the address of that first girl who wrote me. Strange thing is, he said that there was no girl working there named Danielle Donnelly.

Dudley sighed and said, "Now that is really strange alright. But maybe he was just helping her out, because she said she didn't want to deal with you anymore."

Rubbing his forehead, Conner replied, "I thought that for a long time. Then, a while back, I got a letter saying that she was coming through these parts, and could I be in Dry Gulch because she would stop there for a couple of minutes on the way through. Most likely she thought Dry Gulch was nearer me than it was. Matter of fact, I checked the train schedule to see when it came through and jumped on a horse. It took me two days of hard riding to get near Dry Gulch and then, of course, you know what happened when I wound up almost there, but lost my mount to fatigue and had to take your horse." He stopped, took a deep breath and cast a gloomy look at his new friend.

"I know," said Dudley. "Then I come along and throw down on you. Sure makes me sick to think about it."

"As much my fault as it is yours, Dudley. Now she's gone," muttered Conner. "I thought maybe the reason I didn't have her correcting my lessons any more was because she'd had to leave the school for some reason. So, right after I got this drilling through the leg you gave me I wrote a letter?"

"Sure."

"It was to her at the school, but I doubt I get an answer. I mean the train was headed the opposite direction."

"One thing you didn't figure, though," said Dudley.

"What's that?"

"Well, what made you think she was on the train? She never once said she was taking a train. She just said she was passing through Dry Gulch. That's all. Maybe she came by horse or buckboard?"

A gleam was evident in Conner's eyes, but then he said, "Well, I can't imagine a lady like she is traveling any other way but by train. I think she would be too delicate and refined to travel any other way."

Then Dudley, with a knowing smile, said, "Bet you'd give all you got to find a fine lady like that wouldn't you."

THE GIRL WHO RODE INTO A STORM

"All I got and then some. I am telling you there is something about this lady that makes her more special than any woman I ever knew."

"Well," replied Dudley, "let's get you out of this bed. You are good enough to travel now. We'll find this woman. I have an idea how we can start on the trail. I'm going to go with you. I've messed up considerable this little game of yours; now I'm going to do what I can to straighten it out. Sometimes two are better than one. Anyway I'm going to stick with you until you've found her or lost her for good. What do you say?"

Conner replied, "You're pretty straight, but what good does it do for two gents to look for a needle in a haystack? How could we start to hit the trail and find her?"

"Well, we assume she was on that train. I'll buy that as pretty logical based upon the type of woman you say she is. Maybe we could find the Pullman conductor that was on it, and he might remember her. They have good memories, some of those gentlemen. We'll start by finding him, which should be pretty easy to do."

"You know what. You're a pretty smart fellow," offered a delighted Conner.

"Well, we have done the thinking. Now let's do some acting."

"When can you start, Dudley?"

"Well, it will be dark soon. What about first thing in the morning."

"I'll be fit and ready at sun-up."

"Then tomorrow we start."

Dudley headed out the door, looked back over his left shoulder and smiled. Conner noticed something that seemed recognizable in his manner, but he could not put his finger on what it was. What difference did it make? He had found a good friend who was going to ride by his side and hopefully help him find the woman he loved.

Chapter 3
Dudley Was a Wonder Indeed

Robert Stonewall Martin, Pullman conductor extraordinaire with years of forced smiles and a demeanour that commanded respect despite his position as a servant to riders, was a man who had an air of distinction about him. He was ramrod straight with impeccable manners and clothes that matched. He was large and muscular enough to have danced around the ring with John L. Sullivan. There was a dignity to him, and despite being of the black race, he was never discriminated against in Montana, because people there had great respect for him. He had come from Mississippi, where being black was a handicap in the part of the country that could never face the fact it had lost the Civil War and the slaves had been freed. Rob, as he was affectionately called, put his life in the south behind him and made a name for himself as Montana's best Pullman Porter, where he had worked primarily on the Fairview to Billings run, with a stop in Dry Gulch, where he made his home. Each east to west run, he changed with another Pullman conductor and spent two days home, then would take a train back to Fairview when it made its west to east run and spend two days there. He was a man who lived a double life few knew about. In Dry Gulch he had a wife and three kids, and in Fairview he had another wife and two children. Still, he was one of those rare men who carry their dignity with them past the doors of their homes. His home in Dry Gulch, during the short intervals when he was off the trains, was a tiny but tidy shack on a hill above the train station. It was made up of one not overly large living room, and four cubicles for bedrooms with a little alcove adjoining to the far right of the living room; but Rob had seized the opportunity to hang a curtain across the alcove, and, since it was large enough to contain a sofa and a master's easy chair, he referred to it as his den.

He was this particular morning seated in his den, with his feet protruding through the curtains as he rested in the overstuffed chair he cherished, when there was a knock on the door. He surveyed himself in his mirror before he answered it, making sure he was spiffy. Having decided he was sufficiently presentable, he advanced to the door and slowly opened it.

THE GIRL WHO RODE INTO A STORM

He saw before him two men. One seemed a bit rugged, but the other was what some folks would have called effeminate looking with his shiny little boots, silk bandana and shirt with frills on the sleeves. He did not know Dudley, but he knew of him, and he immediately surmised this was the sharp dressed cowboy of whom he had heard much, a man who liked to dress as a dandy, but was slick with cards, fast with a gun and furious with his fists when wronged. There was something about him that impressed Rob. He, like Rob, was dressed with elaborate care. Dudley wore grey spats in his shirt, and his clothes were obviously well tailored with a fit that hugged his slim but somewhat muscular body. On the whole he was indeed a dandy to behold, but there was an air about him that let you know he was not to be trifled with by any man. The handkerchief, which protruded from the breast pocket on the vest he wore showed an edging of red frills and was made of fine linen. He was definitely a dashing-looking fellow. Oh, and the tight-fitting trousers hugged his legs like gloves. So overwhelmed at Dudley's appearance, Rob hardly took notice of Conner.

"You're Mr. Martin, I suppose," said Dudley very softly.

"I am, indeed," said Rob, and, stepping back from his door, he invited them in with a sweeping gesture that seemed almost theatrical, as he said, "Come into my den, where we can sit and be more comfortable. May I get you gentleman a drink perhaps?"

"No thanks," said Dudley, as he eased into a chair, "we are in a bit of a hurry." He then pointed at Conner and continued, "A bit of a hurry, because this fellow is in love, and we think you might be of some help. Mind if we fire a few questions?"

"Certainly not," said Rob. At the same time his demeanour indicated he was arming himself with caution as one could never tell real intent from people with whom you were unfamiliar.

"Truth is," tendered Dudley, as he eased back in his chair and smiled while his dark, perfectly proportioned eyebrows arched a bit, and his brown eyes seemed to glisten in the light filtering through a small window behind Rob, "we are looking for a lady who was probably on the train you got off of a few days ago. We think you may possibly remember her."

"Might at that. You want to describe her. I gotta pretty good eye when it comes to ladies."

"Well, that is the problem," replied Dudley. "We don't really know her looks, but she was coming from the east, so she would have been on your train as it chugged its way toward western Montana." He then looked over at Conner and nodded for him to offer his observations.

"She would have most-likely shown herself to be self-reliant; prideful of her looks a bit I suppose, and if she spoke at all you would probably have assumed she was an educated woman, a very well-educated woman who probably had an air of sophistication about her."

Rob got up, walked over to a desk in the far corner and brought out a ledger. "Let me see here when she woulda been on the train?"

"Thanks," replied Dudley.

Looking down at his ledger, he said, "Well, that is pretty easy then, very easy. Train left Fairview on time, and it was fully loaded – 33 people on the two passenger cars." He scanned the ledger with the precision of a surgeon with a scalpel in his hand, his index finger representing the scalpel. "Nineteen got off in Miles City and four got on. Then in Nichols eight got off to catch the southbound train to Big Sky. That left only ten passengers between there and Dry Gulch. And as I said, I got a very keen eye for faces, but when it comes to pretty faces my memory is sharp as a tack."

His memory was kicking in now, as Dudley and Conner noticed his lips twitching just a bit as he said, "Of, course, it is easy to remember someone when they are the only woman on the train after Nichols. I talked maybe a minute with her. Intelligent acting woman she was and very nice. I mean this ain't Mississippi, but still us coloured folks are generally dismissed as nothing but lowly servants by white folks. She was different though. She had a pleasant smile, and treated me with respect, but yeah, there was just something about her, but doggone it, I can't recollect what it was right now. But for some reason she was different. Physically beautiful lady, but something was different, something different. Can't recall what?"

Conner, on edge now, said, "What do you mean different? I mean come-on, if there was something different about her surely you can recall what it was."

Rob's demeanour took a dramatic turn, as he sensed Conner was a bit of a ruffian, a man who lacked respect for folks of colour. Rob Martin's back stiffened and as he stood by the desk he flipped the ledger down and his opinion of the two sank. His eyes hardened and his breathing became more pronounced.

Sensing a drift in their purpose, Dudley turned to Conner and said, "The gentleman can't recall what it was." He then turned to Rob. "I am afraid my friend is a bit overwrought, as this is very important to him, obviously. Please excuse his curt manner. The point is," went on Dudley gently and calmly, "that my friend is very eager for important reasons to see this lady, to find her. And he doesn't even know her real name. If you can remember anything about her, her name first, then, where she was bound, if anyone was with her, how tall she is, the colour of her eyes, we'd be glad to know anything you could share."

Rob cleared his throat and took on a thoughtful demeanour. "Gentlemen," he said in a determined voice as he took his seat, "I might be setting this lady up for ill intents. I don't know the real purpose why you need this information. It might make me more cooperative if I knew the purpose of your search. The real reasons behind your quest would calm my suspicions."

J. WAYNE FRYE

THE GIRL WHO RODE INTO A STORM

Conner was getting impatient, as was evidenced when he said, "The purpose ain't to kidnap her, if that's your drift. We ain't going to treat her wrong, Mr. Martin. I am an honourable man."

Just as curt, Rob replied, "Honourable is a fancy word, and it can have different meanings according to whose using it. I don't know you mister." He then looked over at Dudley and continued. "You I don't know either, but I know your reputation. You are looked on as a stand-up guy, a bit eccentric in your mannerisms and dress, but an alright person. For that reason, I am allowing you to question me, but I am not accustomed to rudeness from anybody, and just because I happen to be black it shouldn't be assumed I will tolerate rudeness from anybody."

Dudley remained calm as he said, "I apologize if my friend is a bit distraught. This means a great deal to him, and I assure you we mean the lady no harm. I am sure you understand a man's infatuation with a woman. My friend believes he is in love with this woman. They have only met through the mail, corresponding a few times. She wanted to meet him here, and through a set of circumstances beyond his control, he missed the train when it came through. If you could just maybe reflect a bit, think about what you found so unusual about her, maybe it would help us."

"I wish I could remember what it was, but I just can't. I know the lady was almost regal in her appearance, but I just can't recall what it was that made her seem unusual or special beyond that."

THE GIRL WHO RODE INTO A STORM

"Do you remember the colour of her eyes," asked an impatient and somewhat impertinent Conner McCord. "Surely you can remember that if she was so striking. I mean that should be easy enough to recall for anyone."

There was just the shade of a threat in Conner's voice that made Rob Martin bristle. Conner had little understanding for being black in America at this time or any time. What is that old saying, "Do not criticize, ridicule or abuse until you have walked a mile in my shoes." Conner was simply unable, because of his whiteness, to understand what it was like to live in a society where the first thing people notice is your skin colour. Rob Martin had endured prejudice as a child in Mississippi, even having seen his uncle lynched for merely glancing at a white woman. He refused to accept the evil of segregation in the part of America that simply could never get over the fact that it had lost the Civil War and the slaves had been freed. Well, the truth was they had never really been freed in a society that was run by and for white people and it would take a great many years for black people to climb out of the pit of despair that was used to keep them perpetually trapped in a subservient socio-economic class as a result of institutionalized racism. However, Rob Martin was no man's slave, and as an amateur pugilist of much brawn and a good deal of boxing skill, he was not one easily intimidated. He cast a wary eye on Conner in particular, thinking one punch would straighten out his arrogance, and

Dudley, despite his reputation for bravado, just seemed too effeminate acting to put up much of a fight.

"Fellows," Rob gruffly said, "I don't have much time off. This is my day for rest. I have to say good-bye to the both of you."

Dudley stood up and had an air and swagger to him that seemed to be recognizable to Conner, but he just couldn't place it. "I thought so," said Dudley as he looked over at Conner. "Stand by the door Conner and see that nobody steps in and disturbs me as I kick this fellow's butt."

Smiling, Rob said, "You must be kidding you prancing little peacock. Pull your feathers in and get outta my house."

Conner said, "Forget it, Dudley."

"Nope, I am going to argue with Rob in a way he'll understand better than the chatter we've been making so far," he said as he stepped lightly but forcefully forward. "Mr. Martin, you know what we want to find out. Spill it, and spill it now."

A cloud of anger gathered within Rob Martin as he could not believe this dandelion of daintiness in his finery and silk accouterments was standing up to him, standing up physically to a man that was a giant compared to him. It was impossible to believe what was being said, and yet the words still rang there, rang within his head as his anger grew. This was the strangest man he had ever seen, a man with no fear, despite the huge size difference. He almost hated that he was going to have to pulverize this little squirt of a man.

THE GIRL WHO RODE INTO A STORM

"Why you about to meet a fate that will bring you more pain than you ever imagined," burst out Martin, and, stepping in, he leaned forward with a perfect straight left that was lightning fast with his sinewy muscles flexing violently. However, Dudley moved his head just as quickly and ducked under the punch. Punching a hole in thin air took a lot out of the over-sized Rob Martin, and as he sucked for breath Dudley moved in closer with an outstretched right hand, bottom of the wrist flexing outward to hit him solidly in the rib cage, forcing more air out of him, just as he also slammed his high footed boot heel into the front of his ankle.

Conner had once seen a small Chinese man use those techniques against a big brute. It was something called karate, and you used position, hand and foot strength to overcome a size difference. Despite the violence, it was a thing of beauty to behold, almost like a well-crafted ballet.

Another flattened hand hit Rob in the neck, making him cough and gasp for air as he wobbled from side to side. He was out on his feet. In today's fight game, not even a standing eight count would have saved him. Dudley signalled for Conner to help him place the shocked and bewildered Rob Martin back into his easy chair. With Conner's assistance, Dudley dragged the huge, hulking brute of a man to the chair and gently placed him in it. Martin was stunned both physically and mentally that he could be bested by a dandy like Dudley.

THE GIRL WHO RODE INTO A STORM

Presently Rob's dull eyes cleared and filled with amazement as he sank limply back in the chair, aghast with embarrassment and awe of the small man in front of him. He began to stutter out words, "Don't hurt me no more. What is it you want of me?"

Dudley, not showing any cockiness that he had bested a much physically superior man, very politely said, "We want talk, a lot of talk and a lot of true talk. Understand? It's about that girl. I saw you grin when you thought of her; you remember her well enough. Now start talking, and remember this, if you lie, I'll be even more brutal next time. I am a peaceable person," and then he looked over at Conner, "but as my friend here will attest, I am not someone with whom you want to mess."

The eyes of Robert Martin gazed directly into Dudley's eyes and he knew Dudley meant business. He licked his lips and managed to gasp: "Everything I know, of course. I'll tell you everything, word for word. I mean I did learn her name," and then he pointed over at the ledger, "it is writ down right there with all the other passengers that day. I shoulda told you from the start."

"You're doing fine," said Dudley. "Keep it up, and we'll settle this in a peaceable manner."

"We'll get to the name, but first, what did she look like?"

"Soft dark brown hair, brown eyes, her mouth was well, there is an impolite phrase for her lips I won't use, but just say they were pouty and ripe, as if they were ready to give a man some real pleasure."

Conner was not pleased by the impertinence displayed by Rob in describing her lips, but as he bristled with anger, he kept quiet, because he knew there was more vital information to come.

"Don't worry about politeness. You don't have to be polite and lie. We want the truth. How big is she?"

"About five feet and five inches, and maybe a little more weight than normal for someone her size. Not big, though. She carries the weight in all the right places if you get my drift."

Again, Conner felt rising anger, but controlled himself, as Dudley said in his soft, calm voice, "You sure are an expert on the ladies, Martin, and I'll bet you didn't miss her name?"

"Her name?"

"Yep, I told you. It is right there on the ledger."

"You don't need to look at a ledger. You know it. Say it."

"Carmine Jones."

Taking a deep breath, Dudley said, "Did she say anything more, anything about where she expected to be living in the future?"

"I don't remember any more," said Martin sullenly, as he gazed hard at Dudley, still trying to figure out how such a dandy had bested him in fisticuffs. "I didn't sit down and have any long talk with her. She just spoke to me once in a while when I did something for her. I suppose she must be some kind a crook, maybe stole from you?"

Conner interjected, "As we told you, we are bringing her good news of love."

Dudley was not satisfied yet. "Now see if you can't remember where she said she lived? Maybe she lived in Billings?"

Rob blinked and swallowed hard. "The only thing I remember her saying was that she could see the river from where she lived."

"And that's all you know?"

"Yes, not a thing more about her I assure you," replied Rob as he eyed Dudley with sullen malevolence. He could not restrain himself from levelling a threat though, as he continued. "Maybe there'll be a new trick or two in this game before it's finished. I'll never forget you, you fancy pants dandy piece of cow dung." Then he looked at Conner with equally enmity. "And that goes for you, too."

"You have no idea just how fancy I really am," offered a smiling Dudley.

Rob said, "I got a gun, and them fancy moves you make are no good when up against a gun."

Still smiling, Dudley replied, "Mr. Martin, you pull a gun on me, and I'll tattoo your torso with lead from it after I take it away from you, and then I'll finish by shoving it down your throat and make you choke on it if you're still alive."

Conner was impressed with Dudley. He might be a dandy and effeminate acting, but he was one tough hombre with nerves of steal. The two of them walked out, and Conner said as they closed the door behind them, "You are something else."

THE GIRL WHO RODE INTO A STORM

Walking down the tracks back to town, Conner felt proud that he had found such a fine friend. Still, as he looked at him from the side, he couldn't help but think, "I have seen this guy somewhere before."

They boarded their horses and left on the train to Billings. They carefully summed up their prospects and what they had gained. Dudley said, "We started at pretty near nothing. All we knew was she was on this train, a few days ago. Now, we know her name is Carmine Jones, and that she lives where she can see the river out of her window. I guess that narrows it down pretty close, doesn't it, Conner?"

"Close?" asked Conner. "Close, did you say? Well, Billings must be more than 1000 people. And we aren't sure that was where she stopped. I mean the train from Denver leaves from there, too. Suppose she is headed for Denver. Ain't gonna be easy searching every apartment with a view of the river, if she is headed there."

"Don't be so pessimistic. She may be living in Billings, maybe moving there. It is not that big a city. Hey, even if she did go to Denver, then we will pick up her trail in Billings. For smart detectives like us this should be pretty easy. Just take a little shoe leather and time is all. And, what about her looks? Can't be that many women in Billings as striking as she is. I mean this woman will stand out in any crowd. Whether she stayed there or took the train to Denver, we have a good chance of finding someone who saw her."

THE GIRL WHO RODE INTO A STORM

Conner looked at his companion in awe. He had become used to being amazed by Dudley. He reached over and touched his arm. He said nothing, just let him know how much he appreciated all the help. Words were not necessary. Just a look was all it took. Then, Conner looked up at the overhead luggage rack at his small suitcase with a few belongings he had bought at the local haberdasher's, and then stared at Dudley's large trunk. He thought that he must have brought a month's worth of clothes. This guy loved to dress up and he did it in style.

Seeing Conner was worried, Dudley gave him that calm, peaceful, kind smile and said, "Hey, a town's a town, and a river's a river."

Billings was mostly a place where people changed trains to go farther west or to go south to Denver. The two of them had asked the Pullman conductor about a striking lady who would have been on the train a few days before, and if maybe he had noticed her. He was very cooperative and said, "That was one fine looking lady. Said she was going on to Denver. Don't blame you for wanting to meet up with her."

"How long a delay until the train for Denver," asked Dudley."

"Well, this is Friday, so there is a two day wait. Train from the north stops overnight to give the crew a rest. Plenty to do in Billings though. Try the Red Dog Saloon if you want to play some cards. They got a hotel right there. Ain't fancy, but its comfortable and affordable."

THE GIRL WHO RODE INTO A STORM

They checked into the hotel, getting separate rooms. Dudley declined an invitation to go to the saloon. Said he was too exhausted.

Billings, was a pretty wild place, but Conner had seen wilder. The Red Dog was filled as it was a Friday night. He sauntered up to the bar and asked for a beer. The man beside him said, "New in town, uh?"

"Yes, just passing through. Me and my partner are waiting for the train to Denver."

As they were talking, there she was. No, not the woman on the train for whom Conner was looking, but none other than Deanna Defoe walked through the swinging doors like a queen in full regalia. How can one adequately describe a woman like Deanna?

The men in the place suddenly realized that they were in the presence of a raging storm, a tempest of female fury so beautiful that she was like the Mona Lisa come to life. She was a masterpiece painted with the brush of an artist touched by an angel with each stroke so finely formed that you could feel the breath of God himself with every stride she took. This was more than a woman. This was a goddess sent down from on high to walk among mortals. Her body was a temple of amorous worship. It was as if she was fashioned very curiously of roses and silk. The immaculate crispness and smoothness of her stride made each movement forward as graceful as a gazelle. With her stateliness you felt the warmth that flowers must feel when they bloom through the snow, under the first concentrated rays of the sun that introduces spring. Her eyes were dark, dark as chocolate, dark as coffee, dark as the polished wood of fine furniture. They were set in a fair face, oval, like a teardrop. Her easy smile could stop a man's heart. Her lips were red. Not the garish painted red so many women believe makes them desirable. Her lips were simply naturally red, with a freshly licked look that made one desire to taste them, for it appeared as if she had just eaten strawberries and left a bit of the nectar on those luscious lovely puffy mantles of desire. She was not loud, nor vain. A person stares at a fire because it flickers, because it glows, because it gives off warmth. There was a light about her, a glow that made you tingle with desire.

Conner was in search of another woman, but this woman fascinated him like no other. Yet, he knew she was way out of his league. That was why he had not spoken to her all those days watching her play poker. No, she was way beyond him, beyond any hope he might have to curry her favour.

She reminded him of being on ice. Go out in the early days of winter, after the first cold snap of the season. Find a pool of water with a sheet of ice across the top, still fresh and new and clear as glass. Near the shore the ice will hold you, but slide out farther and farther. Eventually you will find the place where the surface just barely bears your weight. There you will feel what Conner felt. The ice splinters under your feet. Look down and you can see the white cracks darting through the ice like scurrying ants headed back to their queen. It is perfectly silent, but you can feel the sudden sharp vibrations through the bottoms of your feet. You know it is dangerous, but there you stand, not moving, just relishing the danger. That is what happened when Deanna looked over at Conner and smiled. His heart raced like a freight train speeding down a hill into a valley where sunflowers kissed the morning sun. Upon this breeze of desire, Deanna spread her glory like a thousand gentle knots tied into soft bows of delight and a sweet light beyond all radiance danced in her glittering brown eyes where heaven on earth had taken up residence. She moved gracefully beside Conner and said, "I recognize you from Dry Gulch. My name is Deanna. Want to buy me a drink? I mean all that time in Dry Gulch you spent staring at me should warrant just one drink, don't you think?"

"I, I, I" muttered a dumbfounded Conner.

"Get hold of yourself now. I won't bite. Well, at least not until we get to know one another better."

"I, I, I" again muttered Conner, unable to put an intelligible sentence together.

Giggling, Deanna said, "Now, just calm down and tell me your name. Come on. It isn't hard."

She raised her dainty right index finger to her thick, succulent, puffy lower lip and gently tapped on it as she said, "this is called a mouth. You use it to speak, and it can say more than the word *I*, so come on now, show little Deanna that you are a big boy and can speak in complete sentences."

THE GIRL WHO RODE INTO A STORM

As everyone in the saloon looked with envy at Conner, he said in almost a whisper to Deanna, "I am so sorry. I am not accustomed to attention from such a beautiful woman."

"Well, if you play your cards right, you might get more attention that you ever thought possible. Come on now, your name."

"It's Conner – Conner McCord."

"See, that wasn't hard, was it?"

"No," replied Conner, as he took a deep breath and seemed to be getting himself under control. "I would be delighted to buy you a drink."

"Well, thank you. That would be nice. I know it is not very lady-like, but I am not feeling very lady like tonight, so I think I'll have beer."

Conner signalled the bartender for two beers, and the two of them stood there for almost two hours sharing drinks as Conner began to relax, feeling comfortable with her. Then she asked him a question he wished she hadn't. "So, the rumour is you are looking for a certain lady."

"How did you know?"

"I know a lot of things. I am a pretty perceptive and intuitive woman."

It was obvious to Conner she was, like Dudley, a well educated person. It made him wish even more that he had finished that correspondence course to improve his vocabulary, but it did not seem to bother her that he was far less articulate that she was. This was a refined lady, but a woman, who, obviously, was not one to look down at someone less educated.

THE GIRL WHO RODE INTO A STORM

She leaned in close to him and whispered, "It is getting late, why don't we get ourselves a bottle of rye and go back to your room? You do have a room don't you?"

Almost physically shaking at the thought of wrapping his arms around Deanna, Conner ordered a bottle of rye, and the two of them walked out of the saloon. For the moment, Conner had completely forgotten Carmine Jones.

They walked into Conner's room, and as soon as the door closed, they were wrapped in each others arms. Their lips met and their tongues began a duel of delight. Conner could feel her small breasts against his chest, and as he started to slip his hand under her dress, she said, "Slow down now. I am a young woman, and I have no intention of getting pregnant. I will give you the release you desire, but I will not risk a pregnancy."

She very artfully pushed Conner toward the bed, and what followed was an incredible experience for them both. Conner never dreamed that a woman could stay fully clothed while she removed his pants and give him the greatest pleasure imaginable. After nearly an hour, he lay prone on the bed, and as this mysterious woman stood there smiling down at him, all he could say was, "Thank you."

She giggled a little and as she turned to leave, looking back, she said, "No, thank you. You are probably the sweetest, dearest man I have ever known. I could tell right away that there was something special about you."

J. WAYNE FRYE

THE GIRL WHO RODE INTO A STORM

Almost pleading, Conner said, "I need to see you again."

"You are going to Denver. You need to get your rest, and with me around, you'll get no rest."

How did she know he was going to Denver? Was she part of the mystery about that woman on the train? He couldn't resist. He said, "How did you know I was going to Denver? I didn't tell you that."

"Yes you did, and you told me about the girl who you are undoubtedly in love with."

"No, no."

A worried look of concern descended upon her countenance, as she said, "You were too mesmerized with me to remember what we talked about. I can't help it if I have that effect on men. Who knows, if things don't work out with Carmine Jones, maybe our paths will cross again."

Had he told her Carmine's name? Was he so infatuated that he couldn't really remember what they talked about? No, absolutely not. He knew he had not told her about Denver or Carmine.

She scurried out the door in the blink of an eye. He leaped up, quickly put his pants on and burst into the hallway, and she was gone like she had disappeared into thin air. Overwhelmed with questions, he went down to the desk clerk and asked if there was a Deanna Defoe registered. "No," replied the clerk. Then he asked if he had seen the woman he brought up to his room leave the hotel maybe two minutes ago. Again the reply was, "No."

Conner began to worry. Why was he pursuing a woman he had never seen, when he had just been with one who lit a fire in him that was going to be impossible to put out. Yet, though she had given him a brief interlude of euphoria, she was what he thought to be unattainable. Why, oh why had she given him that moment in the heaven of her arms?

Lock eyes with me so I can see into your soul.
Press your lips against mine so I know your taste.
Lay naked with me, so I know your insecurities.
Sing a song so I know the tune of your heart.
Dance in the rain of hope as we gently part.

The next morning, Dudley knocked gently on Conner's door. For some reason, the light, soft knock made Conner, for a split second, think it might be Deanna. His dejected look, when he opened the door, made Dudley smile and say, "Obviously, you were expecting someone else."

"Sorry friend," offered Conner who ushered Dudley in. "I am afraid I was hoping, yes, for it to be someone else. Last night was a night I shall remember forever, a night for the ages, as I was in heaven in the arms of an angel."

"Well," replied Dudley, "maybe you should share with me the story of this heavenly encounter. I, for one, have never put much store in tales from that thing called a Bible that is filled with more evil than good. Enlighten me."

Conner pointed to a chair as he sat on the edge of the bed. "Have a seat. It'll take awhile."

"No problem. We still have another day before the train leaves for Denver."

Sharing the tale of his encounter with Deanna Defoe obviously piqued Dudley's interest and he said, "This is a woman I need to meet. You make her sound like the most divine creature to ever walk the earth. Are you sure you don't want to pursue her rather than this mysterious Carmen Jones?"

"Ah, I should be so lucky as to encounter her again, but alas, I do not think she would be interested in a real relationship with me."

Eyes beaming with sincerity, Dudley said, "Never underestimate yourself Conner." He then got up, walked over to the window and looked out as he continued, seemingly lost in a dreamlike state. "I have seen the real you. You have a lot to offer any woman. Only once in your life do you find someone who can turn your life around, someone who lights a fire in you that you simply cannot put out. I know from personal experience, so I do not speak from ignorance. It often happens in an instance, in the blink of an eye, or sometimes it is an accumulation of things. It might even start off with ill will between the two, but over time that barrier of ill breaks down and you realize there is something special about that person. You tell them things eventually that you have never shared with another soul and they absorb everything you say and want to hear more. You may even be unable to let them know that you love them, out of fear that you will be rejected."

THE GIRL WHO RODE INTO A STORM

Dudley turned toward Conner, looking at him with absolute sincerity. It was obvious that Dudley carried deep within him affection for someone who had touched his heart. It brought Conner to the realization that a journey into love was fraught with hills, curves and bumps in a road that tried a person's soul. Conner could see the pain of love within Dudley.

Taking a seat across from Conner, and looking into his eyes with sincerity that bored into Conner's brain with words directly from the heart, Dudley's calm, low, soft voice was like a melody paying homage to love. "When the spark of love is kindled within you, it is like the sun that had been behind a cloud bursts forth with a radiance that makes a comfortable flame become a raging fire. The things most people would consider insignificant such as a note, a song, a kind word, a smile, a tear, a knowing nod, a mere touch become magnified a thousand fold. Memories of your carefree childhood come flooding back as you feel young, giddy and irresponsible again. Colours seem brighter and more brilliant. In their presence, conversation is irrelevant, as just being with them, being in close proximity gives you a feeling of fulfillment. You think of this person constantly no matter where you are or what you do. Simple things bring them to mind, like a clear blue sky, a gentle breeze or the feel of warmth from the sun's rays. You open your heart knowing that it could be broken one day, but you have no control. You have no recourse but to love and love and love."

J. WAYNE FRYE

THE GIRL WHO RODE INTO A STORM

Conner's eyes, like Dudley's were moistening now, as he had never seen a person so sensitive, so capable of expressing the emotions of love. He felt a grand affinity for Dudley. He was more than a mere man. He was a poet of passion.

Dudley got up, sighed and ambled over to the window. He again looked out at the dusty street below, watching people scurrying about, stared at the stained glass window in the saloon across the street as the sun's rays bounced off it causing him to squint. He turned back toward Conner who sat enthralled and amazed at Dudley's oratorical skills. There was the pain of love in every word, as if each one bore a tear of affection for someone he carried deep passion for.

Dudley again sat down. "You know you are making yourself vulnerable, but you cannot help yourself. You find strength in knowing that you have found truth in your life, the truth that you will remain forever loyal and devoted to this person until the end of your days. You have found something you have looked for all your life, and life suddenly becomes worthwhile, exciting and filled with devotion for the person who has brought clarity to your existence. Your every hope, your every dream, your every desire is wrapped up in love for this person. You want to know that when the black veil of eternity descends over you the last thing you do will be to look into their eyes and whisper one final time - I love you."

Although he felt embarrassed, Conner could not help himself. He wiped tears from his eyes.

Dudley took a deep breath and shrugging his shoulders, walked toward the door and said, "Let's go have breakfast."

Conner could not speak. He just got up and walked out of the room with Dudley. How, he thought, could any man be so sensitive? One could expect this type of sensitivity from a woman, but never had Conner seen a man so capable of expressing emotion. Dudley was a wonder indeed.

Chapter 4
Worship at the Altar of Greed

The day was spent in leisure as the two friends enjoyed one another's company. Their friendship was blossoming, but Conner kept thinking of Deanna and the incredible night he had with her. It was not about the sex, as that was more or less an afterthought. Rather, it was about the connection the two seemed to have forged, but he felt it was a connection that would not lead to a burgeoning romance, simply because she was so intellectually superior and he had an interest in the girl on the train that also kept nagging at his psyche. He could not just let it go. There was an unexplainable pull she had on him. It might be a fruitless pursuit, but he had to see it through. He had to know why she wanted to see him.

THE GIRL WHO RODE INTO A STORM

Yet, despite his need to follow the girl on the train, he was enthralled with Deanna. He thought that, even though it was a hopeless situation, he needed to also find out just how she really felt. It was obvious that she was pretty ambivalent about sex, and no doubt, saw it as more a recreational activity than a solidification of compatibility. Reflection made him think that Dudley and she were probably more suited for one another, as their similarities were uncanny, and their articulate natures were apparent without reservation.

It was a pleasant day for both men, and since their train was leaving at noon the next morning, Dudley said goodnight a little past eight, but encouraged Conner to get himself a drink in the saloon, and just maybe the woman whom he had talked about all day might show up again. It was worth a try at least.

By ten o'clock Conner was about to give up, when there she was, walking through the swinging doors again with her customary regal manner, displaying beauty that even exceeded the previous night's grand and glorious manifestations that had mesmerized all within her sphere.

Conner's world was now a better place, because she had smiled in it, and she did it directly at him as she did not walk, but glided his way, as all eyes focused on this magnificent creature of loveliness. Her smile was a wink and a nod of recognition toward Conner. He felt a sizzle of raging fire course through his body as his breathing quickened and he stared at her in disbelief.

THE GIRL WHO RODE INTO A STORM

She was providing Conner with a free and infectious gift that radiated from her mouth as muscles in her cheeks tightened and her dimples formed a cherub magnificence to show enjoyment in the simple pleasure of the moment, bringing a sparkle of vigour to Conner who stood in awe of she who now was there by his side. It was as if all the warm light and happiness in the world had just been taken and poured over the stars that light the night sky. However, all that light, warmth and happiness had been poured, not onto the stars, but into Conner's heart.

He felt as though she had been there, standing by that bar, for an eternity, because an infinity of passion can be contained in one moment and this was Conner's moment. He knew that the value of this moment was immeasurable and that if he lived to be a hundred years old there would never be another moment like this one. He was in pursuit of another woman, but that pursuit, even if he found her and wrapped himself in her arms, could never replace what he felt at this single moment in time.

The smile she gave him was not with her lips. It was with her eyes that danced with true delight at seeing him. They sparkled with recognition that Conner was at that moment all she wanted in life. The room was filled with other men, but all she saw was Conner. All Conner saw was her. All the other men about them were staring with envy that an angel had descended from on high to flap her vibrant wings of desire and shine her affection on one lucky man.

THE GIRL WHO RODE INTO A STORM

Conner was watching her talk to him more than he was listening. He was watching her jaw move. She was so precise in collecting her words one-by-one they seemed to spill from her lips. He couldn't understand why he even deserved them. What made him worthy to hear her voice that was melodic, soft and pure with words that floated like soft clouds in a blue sky of hope? He could sense that she worked at making sure she had that voice honed to perfection. She had practiced the art of speaking, refined it into a masterpiece that was painting over the bare plaster walls of his soul.

Smiling at his dream-like state, Deanna, through teeth as white as polished pearls said, "You want to come back down to earth from Mars and take me up to your room where we can sit in peaceful splendour and share a golden moment that will last a life time?"

As they walked across the street, the moon shone down upon the two lovers, basking them in the light of that moment alluded to before, a moment that Conner knew would be fleeting, lasting only briefly and then she would be gone again. Would he spend the rest of his life on the edge of the water of hope looking out to sea as if waiting for his mermaid to appear once again from the depths below the surface, rising to sing a melody of love and passion making each moment he waited as slow and transparent as glass?

As they ascended the stairs she whispered, "You know I will not allow you to do certain things to me, but to you I shall wreck the havoc of passion."

THE GIRL WHO RODE INTO A STORM

She delicately pushed Conner onto the sofa, looked down at him, fell to her knees and slowly unbuckled his pants. He was not just breathing. He was panting like a dog that had chased a cat that leaped high upon a tall fence and all the dog could do was look up at it, wondering how he might somehow get it down. He wanted to touch Deanna in all those soft places that make men wild with passion, but he was afraid to, because he did not want to spoil this moment of glorious ecstasy that made him feel like a Sultan who had picked the loveliest maiden from his harem to enjoy for the night. This was that one moment Conner knew would last a lifetime. Even if he never saw her again, this moment, this one bright shining moment in a lifetime of moments would dance in his memory like a ballet on the stage of life. He was about to enter the nirvana of worship from a woman who, for some unknown reason, found him to be the centre of her world. Moments, oh moments, life is made up of moments strung together to form a whole, but there were some moments that would never be comprehended, understood, even believed. Was he dreaming? How could this woman be slowly removing his pants, grinning with delight as his manhood popped to attention like a flag pole ready to be devoured by a storm of passion. And devoured it was, not in a raging storm, but a storm that put him in the eye of the hurricane with soft billowy clouds on all sides that rested against that pole of pleasure, slowly working back and forth.

He looked up at the ceiling as his eyes rolled back into his head while he floated on a magic carpet of satiated pleasure like he had never experienced before. How long this glorious pleasure continued is incalculable, because they both were lost in the throes of glorious passion that made time irrelevant. Whether five minutes or five hours, it was inconsequentially insignificant, because time for these two stood still.

His body felt like a fine tuned harp under her machinations of pleasure as if her mouth was the fingers of a maestro plucking the strings with precision playing a melody of passion. If people were rain, at this very moment Conner was but a soft drizzle while Deanna was a roaring storm that made the crops grow straight and tall, reaching for the sun that would soon burst forth from the tempest that brought out the life from deep within the earth. He was feeling the coming surge that would not come from the member that was being worshipped, but from his soul. She was sucking his essence from him, but he wanted to give it to her with delight, because it was as if she needed it for survival. He would seed her deep within, depositing his life force so that she could savour his adoration for her womanliness. He exploded!

The moment, the moment, the moment he kept repeating over and over again after he had expended every last bit of energy in his body. He was almost slipping into a coma of euphoric delight when she crawled up beside him and whispered. "I will always treasure this moment."

THE GIRL WHO RODE INTO A STORM

He weakly pulled her to him and they kissed. No, it was not a kiss; it was a union of souls. She, her lips still almost touching his, said, "I have done this many times in many places because of passion and the need to validate myself as a woman. However, I have for the first time found what I can truly love. I have found you. You are my sympathy, my better self, my goodness. I know you seek another, and I understand, but forever I am bound to you. You are a solemn passion conceived in my heart; it leans to you, draws you to my centre and it is the spring of my life, it wraps my existence about you, and, the spark has become a powerful flame, fusing you and me into one. I may perform that ritual that brought you to nirvana with other men in other times in other places, but it will never mean what this meant to me. This moment is irrevocably seared into my soul and will be that which forever abides within me until my last breath."

Conner pulled her tightly into his arms and wanted to do more with her. If he only had the energy he would have torn the garments from her in a fit of passion and pounded her into oblivion, but he simply could not muster the energy. His exhaustion was complete.

She stood before him, looking down at a man who truly knew what it was like to frolic about in heaven. She smiled and said, "I must go my love. Do not rise and walk me to the door. I leave you in sweet repose, satiated and gratified in the glorification of my love and passion for you."

He could not move. He was even unable to make it to the bed. He slept the night on the sofa, drifting off into a slumber that was the most peaceful he had ever experienced. Within his mind he recalled an old poem he had once read:

Soft, my dearest angel stay,
Oh! you suck my soul away;
Suck on, suck on, I glow, I glow!
Tides of maddening passion roll,
And streams of rapture drown my soul.
Now give me one more billing kiss,
Let your lips now repeat the bliss,
Endless kisses steal my breath,
No life can equal such a death.

The pounding on the door was steady and rhythmic, not intrusive. Was it she coming back for more blissfulness in the paradise of passion? No, it was not, although the voice heard was indeed every bit as soft and melodic as Deanna's. Dudley was, indeed, a most unusual man, and when Conner opened the door, he was greeted with a smile as Dudley said, "Well, looks like you had another delightful night."

"If I told you, believe me, you would think I was lying."

"Oh, maybe you should try me. Don't tell me it was that mysterious woman, Deanna, again?"

"It was."

"You know Conner, if I had not heard of her back in Dry Gulch from other men I would say she was nothing but a figment of your imagination. However, others have seen her as well."

"Dudley, I am not sure now whether I should continue my search for the girl on the train or not. I feel I have betrayed her with this woman. Yet, I know this mystery woman is but a mist in the night that disappears when the sun comes out."

Dudley, almost laughing, said, "Maybe she is a vampire and can only come out at night. Did she suck any blood from you?"

Laughing, Conner replied, "She sucked but not blood."

They laughed, went down for breakfast and started on their journey. The train was chugging along toward Denver, but now Conner's mind was on Deanna. As he and Dudley sat across from each other playing cards, two fancy dressed men came into the car and sat near them. They were terribly effeminate, and when they left, Conner said, "A couple of gay blades for sure."

"Are you opposed to love Conner? Who are you to judge?"

"Oh, don't get me wrong. I understand some of us prefer the same sex. I just don't understand why they chose one over the other."

"Maybe they don't have a choice, Conner."

"We all have a choice when it comes to sex."

Dudley eased back in his seat deciding to offer to share a lecture he had heard while in college. "I was once judgemental, because I was reared by religiously devout parents, who frankly would not know Jesus if he bit them on their asses. Their hypocrisy and the hypocrisy of their religious friends drove me from the church forever."

THE GIRL WHO RODE INTO A STORM

"I share your disdain for hypocrisy, my friend."

"You know, I went to college back east, a little place my dear rich uncle had attended called Harvard. Although it was named after John Harvard, a Puritan, it has always encouraged openness and the pursuit of knowledge unencumbered by convention. There are many professors there who refuse to be bound by the constraints of a society that shoves religion down people's throats. I had a very interesting psychology professor who explored sexuality and all its various ramifications on mankind. He believes that a small percentage of people are born with genes that simply make them find the same sex more appealing. Now, when challenged by the more religious students, his reply was that if they were there to promote religion rather than learning, they had picked the wrong class. He saw religion as a barrier to knowledge, because it trapped people in superstition and fealty to a book filled with cruelty."

"I can understand that," interjected Conner. "I find most devotees to Puritanism to be hypocritical, but I am not sure I can countenance men lying with men."

Smiling, Dudley said, "And what about women lying with women. Kind of turns you on, uh?"

Nodding his head positively, Conner admitted that he was right. "Yep, I see your point; I am being hypocritical ain't I?"

"Hey, the first step in stopping your hypocrisy is to recognize it."

THE GIRL WHO RODE INTO A STORM

"You're about the wisest man I have ever known Dudley. In fact, you and Deanna would be more suited to one another than she and I. You both are incredibly intelligent."

"Well, first we'll find your girl who was on the train. Then maybe we'll set out in search of your other mystery woman and see if maybe she would find me as attractive as you."

Laughing, Conner said, "Never happen. Ain't nobody as good looking as me! Now, finish your tale about this professor."

"Well, he just said that there is too little love in the world, and anybody that ridiculed love was not much of a Christian in his book. He said sex was just a recreational activity, and had little to do with love. Now, based upon my observations over the years, I can say he is probably right, but not 100% right. I think it can also be about love, and I have found the best sex was when I had a connection, a real connection with the person. Still, all the whorehouses in this country certainly do attest to it being primarily recreational in nature."

Conner was fascinated with Dudley's knowledge and asked, "What about men who like to dress as women?"

"Well, strange you would ask, because this professor brought in a guest one day. She was a beautiful Indian girl. She talked about her tribe and life on the reservation. She was highly intelligent and had us all mesmerized not just by what she was saying about her life, but by her incredible beauty."

Conner leaned forward showing intense interest. Meeting Dudley had brought him to the realization that he needed to learn more. His admiration for Dudley had stoked a desire to gain knowledge, so that he might one day be as intelligent as he was.

"Truth is this professor is a man way ahead of his time. He then told the class that this was a woman who had the genitals of a male, but that in her mind she was a female. Her tribe, like most Indian tribes before Christians got hold of them was accepting of these types of people. In fact they were venerated and honoured as being special. Of course, the Christians said God does not make mistakes. Frankly, I think his biggest mistake was producing hypocrites like those damn Christians who forced the natives to adopt Christianity by brutalizing them."

The two of them laughed uproariously and Conner said, "I ain't never had no use for finger-pointers. That's why you don't never see me in church. And what causes these people to be that way according to the professor?"

"Well, he wasn't sure, but his opinion was there was something like a birth defect. They were just walking around with the wrong genitals, because in their minds they were another sex. He even said that some day maybe there will be a way to correct that birth defect if medical science is not constrained by the religious bigots who foster hate rather than love."

"That would be nice," offered Conner. "I mean it must be hell stuck in the wrong body."

THE GIRL WHO RODE INTO A STORM

"We all live in one kind a hell or another Conner. I mean look at the hell you went through trying to meet this woman, and the hell I have gone through in my remorsefulness, trying to make things right for my mistake."

"Dudley, you have more than made up for it, and my brashness was part of the blame too. Hey, you are right now on a train with me, helping find that woman, a woman that now I am less sure about, because I have met the most extraordinary woman I have ever known. Yet, I know this new woman simply is way out of my league, despite what you might think. Anyway, she is nothing more than a passing fancy in the night. She pops into my life unexpectedly, and then pops out the same way. How could I ever really know this person?"

"You know her, Conner. You knew her while you sat watching her play poker in Dry Gulch. Sometimes a moment can be an eternity. Sometimes words are not necessary. Sometimes people may connect on a plain in the realm of the unfathomable. Sometimes the connection is brief and transitory, not meant to be truly consummated. Maybe if the real truth, the complete knowledge of this woman was known you would find her abominable, perhaps of a character that was less than stellar, or maybe she is fleeting in your life because she is also afraid just like you are, afraid that if you really knew her that you would find her actually less appealing than you imagine. Maybe you should concentrate on Carmine Jones and forget about Deanna."

THE GIRL WHO RODE INTO A STORM

"You really believe that? I mean you believe Deanna is only toying with me?"

"No, absolutely not. I think she is attracted to you, but Deanna is more a dream than reality. I have heard of her for years, but there never seems to be any permanence. From Dry Gulch to Fairview, I have heard of this beautiful woman with a devil-may-care attitude, uncanny gambling skills, the ability to sit astride a horse as good as any man, a demeanour that is as regal as a queen, but still she has the common touch of humility and an acerbic tongue that can cut a man down quicker than a skilled gunslinger in the street at high noon. Maybe this Carmen Jones is as unreal as Deanna, but I think not. I think you need to remember your time with Deanna and treasure it, as I am sure she treasures your interludes. Life is made up of a collection of moments that are not ours to keep. The pain we encounter throughout our lives comes from the illusion that some moments can be held onto. Clinging to people and experiences that were never ours in the first place is what causes us to miss out on the beauty of the miracle that is the here and now." He waved his hand in a sweeping motion pointing out the coach full of people. "All of this is yours, and none of it is yours. Everything is fleeting. A fleeting moment can become an eternity. From a past encounter everything may disappear in the dungeon of forgetfulness with time. A few furtive flashes or innocent twinkles may be all that survives. Some immaterial details may remain marked in our memory, forever. A significant look, a certain colour or an unforgotten gesture may abide, indelibly engraved in the mind, but nothing is permanent in this thing we call life, because everything can change in the blink of an eye."

Conner at that moment, knew he could never completely put Deanna out of his mind, but he also knew that she was, indeed, truly unattainable. With determination, he said to Dudley, "So, Carmine lives along a river. The South Platte River runs though Denver. Think it will be hard to find her?"

"A river is a river, my friend. Denver is a big town, but there is but one river, and somewhere along that river is a house or an apartment that looks out over the water. Why Conner, she is as good as found."

"Don't know Dudley. Been there once and it's a mighty big place. The river runs a long way through there, and Jones is a pretty common name."

"Yep, but from her description, she is not very common looking. Come on, don't get discouraged."

That night neither of them slept very well, for every rattle and sway of the train was telling them that they were rocking along toward an impossible task in so many ways. Denver was a big town, and there were lots of small cities all along the South Platte River. Maybe she had just said Denver for a point of reference as everyone was familiar with it.

THE GIRL WHO RODE INTO A STORM

Through breakfast in the dining car they were mostly silent. Conner noticed people looking at Dudley in all his finery and Dudley also obviously observed it. He smiled at Conner and said, "Don't let it worry you. I am used to it. I am who I am, and if they don't like it then they are the ones who have to deal with it. I am not going to pattern my dress to suit others. It suits me, and that is all that matters."

"I wish I could be more like you, Dudley."

"No you don't," said the almost tearful Dudley. "I am not the overly confident person I seem. I have my insecurities like everyone else, but I hide them better than most."

Still, Conner wondered about Dudley, because he had such a familiar face. It was a nice face, a soft, kind, caring face. However, he had seen the bad side of Dudley, and he was definitely not one you wanted to get on the bad side of anytime, anywhere. Conner was comfortable with Dudley, but he noticed others looking strangely at him out of the corners of their eyes the minute he turned away or passed them. Was there something about Dudley he was missing?

Dudley noticed a concerned look on Conner's face. He grimaced just a bit and said, "Conner, I can punch a gent for cussing me, or stepping on my foot, or crowding me, or sneering at me, or talking behind my back, or for a thousand other things. But why fight a low life cretin for laughing at you behind your back. It's the one thing not worth answering back except with your own

J. WAYNE FRYE

laughing or with total disregard. Even a dog gets sort of sick inside when you laugh at him, and a man is a lot worse. You may want to destroy the person who is laughing at you, and sometimes you may want to hide from those who point fingers of condemnation. In this world I am who I am, you can take it or leave it, but do not call me out to my face, because then I will not tolerate the disrespect." He paused for a few seconds, collecting his thoughts and continued. "I mean people look at my spats, the red rim of my handkerchief sticking out of my pocket, and that soft gray hat, when I have it on. Well, guess what. I like those things. They make me feel good. I know people call me a dandy. Guess what? I don't give a good goddamn."

Their conversation was cut short by the gradual appearance of a drift of stately-looking houses all in a row, and then more and more. They could look out on block after block of roofs packed close together, or occasional big business structures, as they reached the uptown area and pulled into Central Station.

Denver had just started using a new-fangled invention called street cars, and the two men were thrilled at taking their first ride ever on such a modern contraption. Dudley asked the conductor where accommodations might be found. The conductor swallowed a smile that left a twinkle about his eyes as he surveyed Dudley up and down. "What kind of a place? They got places from fifty cents to fifty bucks a night."

"Fifty dollars might be a bit out of our price range. Let's find something around a dollar or two," said Dudley.

"Tell you what pal," said the conductor, becoming suddenly friendly, "I can fix you up. I know a neat little joint where you'll be as snug as a bug in a rug for $1.50 a night. Really nice."

He pointed out a place at the next stop and said, "Tell the desk clerk Art sent you, and he'll treat you right. And tell him I said $1.50."

The building was old, but neat. The lobby was not elaborate but tolerable. When they said Art had sent them, the clerk, named Bill, said, "And how much am I supposed to charge, according to Art?"

"$1.50," said Conner.

"Damn, Art gives my rooms away cheap. If you take two rooms, it's a deal."

Dudley looked over at Conner and said, "Sounds good to me. My buddy here probably snores."

"I'll make you right to home here, friends."

Bill helped carry their suitcases and led the way down a hall dimly lit by two flickering gas jets. He showed them their respective adjoining rooms, which, much to their surprise had in-room baths.

Dudley closed his door and walked over to Conner's room as Bill said "Why not have a sociable drink fellas? I'll bring up a bottle of rye, on the house?" Then as he left, he looked back over his shoulder and said, "Be right back."

Upon returning, Bill took a seat in Conner's room and the three began to socialize as Bill willingly poured generous drinks. "So, you fellas from Montana. We get lots of folks here from there."

Conner started to lift his glass, but Dudley reached over and stopped him, and said to Bill. "How come you aren't pouring yourself a drink?"

Bill, a chubby man with a gregarious nature, replied, "Never touch it."

Dudley got a serious look on his face, which was a reminder to Conner that there was something bothering him, and a revelation was about to occur. Then Dudley, without any hesitation, said, "You're a liar Bill. I smelled whiskey on your breath downstairs. A man with the early evening breath of whisky I would say is most likely a pretty heavy drinker."

Bill leaned back and sighed, put his hands by his side as he stared directly at Dudley. His whole big body seemed to be wilting, as though in a terrific heat. "I dunno!" he murmured. "I dunno what's got you out of sorts. I tell you, I never drink."

"You are lying. I know it and you know it," retorted Dudley. "I know the smell of whiskey on a man's breath. Played too much poker and bellied up to the bar too often to not recognize it."

"Listen here," replied a belligerent Bill, "You queer-looking sissy dandy. You don't come into my place and call me a liar."

Conner put down his glass on the table and stared at Bill. "My friend here is a man who don't mince words. He tells it like it is, and your nasty remarks about him I will not tolerate."

THE GIRL WHO RODE INTO A STORM

Bill hurriedly, gasping for air, said "I may have taken a small bracer to start the evening. In fact, think I did. That's all. Why make it a big deal?"

"I am not sure," replied Dudley. "I just find it a bit strange that Art sends us here. Looking back on it now, it seems he was definitely overly friendly to strangers. I asked him about a place, but he actually came up to us on the trolley, just stood there waiting for us to start a conversation."

The stare from Bill was intense and the movement of his hand toward the inside of his coat breast pocket indicated he might be reaching for a gun and Dudley said, "Don't put that hand inside your coat. It would be a mistake."

Under the astonished eyes of Dudley and Conner he turned pale, a sickly greenish pallor and his eyes rolled back into his head, and his one hand on the table began to shake.

"Open the window," he said. "The air, it's stuffy in here."

Conner said, as he started to get up. "I'll get him some water."

"No," said Dudley as he pushed the drink Bill had poured over to him. "Drink it, or I'll come over there and take that gun your hiding in your breast pocket out and beat your lying face to a bloody pulp with it."

Shaking, Bill picked up the booze and drank it, slamming the glass back down on the table and looked with intense hatred at Dudley.

"He looks like he's dying," pleaded Conner.

"Then he has killed himself," offered Dudley.

"Gents," began Bill feebly as he gasp for air, slumped over and fell to the floor in a faint. In astonishment and horror, Conner also gasped for air in a room that now seemed stuffy to him as well, but Dudley very calmly went to Bill's side, knelt down and felt his heart. "He's not dead" he said, "but he'll be tolerably sick for a while. Now come along with me."

"But what's all this mean?" asked Conner in a whisper, as he picked up his suitcase and hurried after Dudley.

"Doped booze," said Dudley, without hesitation.

They hurried down the stairs and came out onto the street. There, Dudley dropped his suitcase and quickly dived into a dark nook to the left of the hotel entrance. There was a brief struggle with someone in the nook. Dudley came out, pushing a skulking figure before him, with the man's arm twisted behind his back. It was the streetcar conductor.

"I thought so!" muttered Dudley. "The miscreant was waiting for a signal from the desk clerk that we were knocked out from the doped drinks."

Dudley and Conner grabbed the man between them, rushed him to the steps to the right and flung him headlong down. There was a crashing fall, groans and then silence. Dudley looked down at him and said, "Buddy, you messed with two wrong hombres this time. We may not be from the big city, but we are from the big sky country, and we handle crooks like you in a manner that makes you think twice before you try to hoodwink somebody again. You are getting off easy this time."

The guy turned over, looked up and said, "You queer dandy, I'll dance on your grave."

Conner, filling with rage at the man's remarks, put his foot on his chest and said, "This fella is more man than you'll ever be. One more word and I'll do a dance, too, a dance of death across your chest with my boots."

Dudley reached over and put his right hand gently on Conner's left arm. You could see the emotion in his eyes as he said, "Thanks Conner, but this fellow is not worth killing. He is the kind of low life who works his way through life by taking and never giving. This is a world that slides every day into the kind of greed practiced by people like him. One day all these people will be lined up by the poor whom they steal everything from and dispatched into the black hole of hell where they all belong, but let's not sully our hands by killing this pile of cow dung."

They picked up their suitcases and walked out from the darkness of a sinister place where the malevolence of greed was practiced by men of ill intent, but the truth was, there was no way to ever really walk away from this evil in a nation that worshiped at the altar of greed.

THE GIRL WHO RODE INTO A STORM

Chapter 5
In Some Serious Trouble

They did not refer to the incidents of that odd reception until they had located a small hotel for themselves, only a few blocks away. They procured two pleasant rooms, clean and to their surprise, when they bathed and went down to the lobby there was a new-fangled invention being used on a huge chandelier that hung overhead. It was called the electric light and the hotel was one of the first on the new city power-grid. As they meandered into the bar, Conner said, "What gave you the tip Dudley that we were being set up for robbery?"

"In my business you learn to watch faces, Conner. Suppose you sit in at a game of poker. One gent says everything with his face, while he's picking up his cards. Another gent doesn't say a thing, but he shows what he has by the way he moves in his chair, or the way he opens and shuts his hands. When the conductor approached us, I think he could tell by the way I was dressed that we might be good marks. Right after that he got terribly friendly, and said he could steer us to a friend of his that could put us up for the night pretty comfortable. Well, it wasn't hard to put two and two together. Not that I figured anything out right away.

Conner thought on it for awhile and said, "I'd be a pretty desperate character without you, Dudley."

"Don't underestimate yourself. You are a smart fellow, just haven't been exposed to the seedy side of life as much as I have. Hey, I have been making my living basically playing poker since I was 15. You learn a lot. I may have gone to college, but my real learning has been in the college of life."

They talked for awhile until Dudley said, "Well, I am off to bed. We'll start tramping up and down the river tomorrow early. I mean this has been a pretty trying day. What about you?"

"I think I will stick around awhile, maybe even play a hand of poker."

"Good luck," said Dudley, pushing his right hand through his long dark hair. The pony tail he kept it in added to his dandy looking nature while it fluttered about as he headed upstairs.

Conner asked a group of men at a table if they minded if he joined the game as long as the stakes weren't too high. The dealer pointed to a vacant chair and said, "Take a seat; we ain't playing for big stakes."

After a few hands, Conner had lost maybe $20, but the loss quickly faded from his mind when a complete quiet fell over the place as if some magician had magically waved his hand and said "abracadabra" and the greatest magic trick ever performed had just been manifested before those in the saloon. The trick was making an angel materialize seemingly from nowhere. Conner looked up from his cards and the palpitations in his heart were pounding like kettle drums. There, striding toward the bar was an angel of light sent by a god Conner did not believe in to flap her wings of desire among mortals who could but bow before her magnificence. Her body was a harmonious melding of the imaginations of every great artist who had put the beauty of a woman on canvas. The radiance she gave off was like a tsunami roaring ashore on an island, bringing devastation that was dangerous but beautiful. Her cheeks were lit to a lovely flame, like the thrilling flush of children after their baths in the evening. Her fine forehead sloped gently up to where her hair, bordering it like an armorial shield, burst into lovelocks and waves that accentuated its dark lustre. Her eyes were bright, big, clear, moist and shining with passion for life and the knowledge that she could slay a man with the blink of an eye or a devilish grin that penetrated the heart like a bullet from a Colt 45. Her body hovered delicately with each stride she took.

THE GIRL WHO RODE INTO A STORM

Conner and the other men were nearly breathless in awe. As he put down his cards and said, "I fold," he got up and remembered an old poem he had once read:

Upon the breeze she spread her dark hair
that in a thousand gentle knots was turned,
and the sweet light beyond all radiance burned
in eyes where now that radiance is rare;
and in her face there seemed to come an air
of pity, true or false, that I discerned:
I had love's tinder in my breast unburned.
Was it a wonder if it kindled there?
She moved not like a mortal, but as though
she bore an angel's form, her words had then
a sound that simple human voices lack;
a heavenly spirit, a living sun
was what I saw; now, if it is not so,
the wound's not healed because the bow goes,
and from within my affection flows.

As he walked up to her, he uttered the name that flowed from his lips like fine wine poured into the finest crystal, "Deanna."

That familiar grin creased slowly across her lips as she spoke, not from her mouth, but from her heart, "Conner."

"What are you doing here?"

"I am in Denver on business Conner, and I just happened to check into a hotel where the desk clerk had me sign a register, and low and behold, the name right above mine was scrolled in bold writing that tickled my libido and seared my soul – Conner McCord, and this is the nearest saloon."

THE GIRL WHO RODE INTO A STORM

"You are a vision of loveliness," said Conner.

"Stop making a girl blush," replied Deanna.

The bar was as quiet as a tomb as all eyes were trained on Deanna. She whispered to Conner, "Let's go up to your room where we can relax and talk free of prying eyes and ears, unless, of course, your friend Dudley is sharing it."

"No, I am alone."

Smiling, she took his arm and said, as they walked out of the saloon, "Not for long."

Conner had never known a woman as guarded with her body as Deanna. She appeared to be the most opened mind woman he had ever known, but she guarded her body like it was a gold mine that only she had the map to. She willingly plied her adoration for him, but always stopped short of giving him that which all men crave as if it were the very thing that would keep Conner longing for more, longing to never let go of a woman that was as mysterious as a cat on a hot tin roof.

She lay naked, except for her bloomers, in his arms with her small, soft breasts pressed against his chest. He fell asleep feeling he had a grasp of the real heaven.

Conner awakened and she was gone, but she left a brief note which read: *In your arms I am whole as a woman. You have brought me delight that I never dreamed possible, but your destiny lies with that girl who was on the train which fate made you miss. Find her and find a life that you deserve my dear Conner. We are but two ships passing in the calm, peaceful night, sailing together for a short and glorious time, but ultimately bound for different ports.*

He dressed and hurried to the hotel where he and Dudley had first registered and the clerk nervously pleaded with him not to do him harm, but disregarding his pleas, he simply grabbed the register and looked at it, trying to see what room he had assigned Deanna. She was not listed He described her, pleading with the clerk to give him her room number.

"There was no such woman here, I saw no such woman. Please, please do not harm me," he pleaded.

Shrugging his shoulders, Conner walked out, dejected and heartbroken. He strolled back to his hotel, with a heavy heart. Maybe she was right he thought. Perhaps they were two ships passing in the night headed for different ports. Maybe it was time he realized Deanna was more an illusion than reality.

He did not even mention to Dudley that he had seen Deanna once again. Dudley insisted that they simply walk over the whole area by the river, so as to become fairly familiar with the scale of their task. They managed to make the trip before night and returned to the hotel, footsore from the task that was taxing their mental and physical abilities.

Two very gloomy and silent men ate their dinner that night and went to bed early. But in the morning they began the actual work of their campaign. It was arduous labour. It meant interviewing in every district one or two storekeepers, and asking the mail carriers for Carmine Jones' residence. In spite of all their efforts to appear casual there was something too romantic in this search for a girl to remain entirely unnoticed. People whom they asked became excited and offered them a thousand suggestions. Everybody it seemed had somewhere, somehow, heard of a beautiful woman living in their neighbourhood.

The two intrepid detectives ran down a thousand false clues and found at the end of each something more ludicrous than what had gone before. Maiden ladies they found; and they discovered, at the ends of the trails on which they were advised to go, young women who were ugly, pretty and in-between.

Finally, after three arduous days, they got the first real clue, as they were talking to a pawn shop operator. His eyes lit up when they described the girl, but he said, "Nope, not familiar with her I am afraid."

Then a strange thing happened when, as Conner and Dudley walked away, Dudley looked back over his shoulder and saw the man frantically locking up his store and heading in the opposite direction down the street.

Dudley grabbed Conner's arm and said, as he turned around, "Quick, that store owner just locked up and left in a hurry. He knows something. Come on. We are following him."

Conner, greatly excited, and now having given up on ever connecting with Deanna again, obeyed, and they hurried down the street. They were shocked to see that the man had disappeared into a crowd of people rushing down the street.

"What do you think?" said Conner.

"He has gone to tell somebody, somewhere, that we're looking for a woman named Carmine Jones," he said as he looked at a cabbie furiously whipping his horse headed in the opposite direction with the shop owner sitting in back.

"Come on!" he bellowed as he stepped quickly out to the curb and hailed a passing cabbie. "Follow that cabbie and keep a block away from it," he ordered.

They passed through various areas of the city in clandestine pursuit of the shop owner, and on First Street they turned and darted sharply south for a good dozen blocks, then went due east and came to a halt near the corner of Wynkoop and 17th Street as the cabbie looked back into the coach through the opening and said, "He stopped at what looks like an cul-de-sac down off 17th."

Dudley and Conner stepped from the cab, paid the cabbie and dismissed him with a word of praise for his fine tailing. They stepped around the corner. What they saw was a little street closed at the end and only two blocks long. It had a serene, detached air to it with rows of neat big houses standing majestic but solemnly as a testament to affluence for the most part. There was a bridge across the river in the distance, but where they stood everything seemed surreally cut off from the outside world.

THE GIRL WHO RODE INTO A STORM

The cab which they had been pursuing was drawn up on the right-hand side of the street, looking south, and, as they saw it waiting there its passenger darted up a flight of steps and banged the knocker. The door opened, but they could not see who opened it. The shop owner was allowed to enter. And, as he stepped across the threshold, he drew off his cap with a touch of reverence which seemed totally out of keeping with his character that he had displayed when they spoke to him.

Dudley, brushing his right hand over his long pony tail while rubbing his chin with his left hand, said, "That house harbours someone who knows Carmine Jones, and that somebody is being told excitedly by that shop owner that we are looking for her."

Presently they saw the man coming down the steps and get in the waiting cab. Even at that distance it could be seen that he was smiling broadly, and that he was intensely pleased with himself for whatever he had just done. He had money in his hands.

Dudley said, "He goes and tells whoever is in that house that he's taken us off the trail. They not only thank him, but they pay him for it."

Conner said, "I am tired of pussyfooting around. I am going up there, knock on that door and ask for Carmine Jones."

"Try it," offered Dudley.

Dudley stood at the bottom of the steps as Conner leaped up them to the front door of the house and knocked on the door. He was surprised when it was opened by a stern looking middle-aged man with a beak for a nose. The man levelled a 45 at Conner and said as she slammed the door in his face, "Get outta here."

Dudley could not help laughing, as he observed Conner nearly falling down the stairs, limping a little in his mind with wounded pride. He said to him, "what happened?"

"That nasty man, after I asked him nice and polite if a lady named Carmine Jones was in the house, slammed the door in my face. Damn, I never seen such an ugly looking man, and his disposition matched his looks."

Still smiling, Dudley said, "Look across the street and tell me what you see."

Looking up and down the street, Conner said, "What? I see nothing."

Dudley pointed directly at a sign in a window at the house across the street. In bold letters, it said, *"Room for Rent."*

Conner nodded his head, and said, "So, we check outta the hotel and rent that room. Hope you don't snore."

"That's our room, partner, and right at the front window over the street one of us is going to keep watch day and night, until we make sure that Carmine Jones does or doesn't live in that house."

They secured a big double room that ran across the whole length of the house. From the back it looked down on the river and in the front the windows overlooked the house they had under surveillance.

THE GIRL WHO RODE INTO A STORM

They took up a rotating vigil. For four hours one of the two sat observing the house across the street, and then the other would take up the post. Very few buggies or horses came into the street, and every person who dismounted from one of them had to be scrutinized with diligence. Once a girl, young and slender and sprightly, stepped out of a cab and ran lightly up the steps of the house. Dudley caught his friend by the shoulders and dragged him to the window. "What do you think?"

"Nope."

"Thought so, but wanted to make sure. Sorry I woke you."

Nothing more happened that night, though even in the dull, ghost hours of the early morning they did not relax their vigil. But all the next day there was still no sign of Carmine, no one who came near fitting her description.

Was the place a harmless rooming house of fairly good quality? Not a sign of Carmine appeared even during the second day. By this time the nerves of the two watchers were shattered by the constant strain, and the monotonous view from the front window was beginning to wear on them.

"It's proof that she ain't there," said Conner. "Here's two days gone, and not a sign of her. It sure means that she ain't in that house, unless she's sick in bed. I have two mystery women I love. One is a will-o-the-wisp coming in and out of my life in a frivolous manner, even telling me the last time I saw her to move on which I did, but now I have an even more complex woman I am pursuing. I'm telling you Dudley," he said through laughter, "I'd have better luck pursuing you."

Looking directly at Conner, Dudley replied with a smile, "That kind of stuff is illegal most places."

Although frustrated from the lack of luck, the two decided to stay there for one week to see if Carmine came out of the house across the street. If not, they would conclude that they had misread the intentions of the shop owner.

The third day passed and then the fourth, dreary days of unfaltering vigilance on the part of the two watchers. And on the fifth morning even Dudley sat dejected with his head in his hands at the window, peering through the slit between the drawn curtains which sheltered him from being observed at his spying. When he called out softly, the sound brought Conner, with one long leap out of the chair where he was sleeping, to the window. There could be no shadow of a doubt about it. There stood the radiantly beautiful Carmine Jones in the doorway of the house. Walking out onto the stoop, she closed the door behind her and paused there looking up and down the street.

Conner snatched his hat and plunged through the doorway like a bullet shot out of a gun. So swift was he that Dudley simply stood by the window, not following him across the street. Anyway, Conner was running so rapidly toward Carmine that even a fine mount under Dudley would have made it impossible to keep up.

Carmine, as Conner raced toward her, knew immediately who it was as she stood in compete shock. She was a beautiful woman with a grey hat that had the brim slightly bent over her forehead. Her dress was tailored grey tweed. There was a pronounced distinction between their clothes, and their looks, as the fine modeled prettiness of her features and the big, careless chiselling features of Conner could not be more different. Dudley saw in her demeanour marked surprise and an element of contrived disdain, as Conner politely removed his hat. He made a long, slow, gangly step closer to her, with both his hands outstretched as Dudley noticed her glance over her shoulder and back at the house from which she had just come. Dudley followed that glance, and he saw, all hidden but for the dark profile of the face, a gangly man mostly in silhouette form. He was standing at an opposite window and gazing scornfully down at what was happening on the stoop of the house.

The man stepped more into the light, and that horrid face filled Dudley, in an instant, with such fear and hatred, such loathing and such dread, such scorn and such terror that he felt a chill overwhelm him. The man's nose was hooked like a bird of prey; the eyes were long and slanting with arched, devilish eyebrows that spoke of something sinister. The face was thin, almost fleshless. One could look at him and detect an emptiness of heart, a soul devoid of empathy or compassion. This was a person whom you absolutely knew not only embraced evil, but thoroughly enjoyed it. This was a man who celebrated malevolence.

THE GIRL WHO RODE INTO A STORM

As for the girl, the sight of Conner seemed to fill her with dread. She shrank back from him to the point of even taking a step up one of the steps of the stoop. Dudley noticed her head shaking, as she denied Conner the right of advancing farther.

One could see within Conner's eyes a pleading for recognition. As he stumbled over words, Dudley could read her lips as she said, "Please do not bother me."

Still, despite urging him to leave, there seemed hesitation in her mannerisms as if she were on the verge of following him, while he shrugged his shoulders and turned away. It was almost as if she wanted to bring him back, for she made a slight outward gesture with one hand, the one that could not be seen by the man in the window. However, if there was a moment of hesitation, it vanished almost immediately, as she hurried off down the street as Conner crossed to the other side.

Defeated spiritually, Conner walked ramrod straight back across the street, but Dudley knew it was all show for him, because Conner did not want him to think he was less than a man. Dudley turned gloomily away from the window and listened to the progress of Conner coming up the stairs. What a contrast between the ascent and the descent. He had literally flown down to Carmine. Now his heels clumped out a slow and regular death march, as he came back to the room.

When Dudley opened the door he could see that Conner had never dreamed he would be treated with such contempt by someone who had actually

J. WAYNE FRYE

asked to see him on her way through Dry Gulch. In the very moment of seeing her, although she was now his second choice, she was still a dream girl, but he had lost her, too and had no hope of ever getting her or Deanna. He had given up on Deanna, because she was so far beyond him that he knew there was no chance, but he really felt that Carmine was a possibility. He walked in, collapsed onto the chair by the window and sighed deeply, as Dudley took a seat on the bed.

After that, Conner did not move so much as a finger from the position into which he had fallen limply. Dudley got up and walked across to him, and laid a kind hand on his shoulder. Dudley's heart felt for him as he said, while still touching him, "I cannot find any words to let you know how sorry I am Conner."

"It's over," said Conner faintly. "I've just wasted a pile of good money-making time from my work, that's all."

"Look me in the eyes and tell me you want to quit."

Sighing, Conner replied, "Hey, I make no secret with you that my first inclination is to be with Deanna, but you and I both know she is out-of-reach. She is a mystery that will never be solved."

"Maybe she would like to have you too, Conner, but perhaps there is something about her that you don't know yet, a mystery that keeps her on the periphery of relationships. It is pretty clear she is attracted to you, but there obviously is something that makes her wander in and out of your life."

"Yes and now Carmine Jones has also wandered out of my life apparently."

"That's where you and I don't agree! Why Conner look at the way things have gone! You've followed her, tracked her clear from Montana to here, and you've given her a chance to see your own face. You can't give up yet."

"Do you know what she said when I come rushing up saying: I'm Conner McCord!"

"What?"

"That she didn't even remember my name."

"What about the letter she sent to you. Did she deny that too?"

"Said I was crazy. And she kept looking back at that house."

"That is because there is someone in that house she is afraid of. There was a guy standing up there at a window watching her and how she acted. My guess is that he is the guy who made her fear signing her real name when writing you. He's the one who has kept her in that house. He's the one who knew we were here watching. Conner, what that girl told you didn't come out of her own head. It came out of the head of the one she is afraid of. The fear of that fellow was too much for her. My guess is there is something very nefarious going on, and we have to find out what it is, or we will never forgive ourselves for deserting someone who is obviously in a very dire circumstance. Right now it is not about a relationship with that girl. It is about helping someone out who is apparently in some serious trouble."

Chapter 6
We've Got Him

"You really believe that she might be in danger," offered Conner.

"I do, and it will take maximum effort from us to get to the bottom of this."

The two resumed their vigil with new determination. However, exhausted from the trauma, Conner fell asleep on the sofa but Dudley sat at his window staring across the street at that house, determined to get to the bottom of the mystery, despite feeling that Conner was chasing two wrong women. Caroline was an enigma, and so was Deanna, but Dudley was sure, beyond any doubt, that Deanna loved him desperately, but there was something that kept her from revealing her true self. Deanna was more like a shadow in the night that just always seemed to float in and float out without any consistency, or was she consistent in her method of appearing just at the most opportune times? She definitely was consistent in showing up to make her unusual kind of love to Conner and then vanish.

Dudley looked over at the peacefully snoring Conner. He was one of the handsomest men he had ever encountered, but he was incredibly naïve. Dudley sighed and thought about how impetuous he had been to challenge his honesty. Why, he considered, had he lost his temper so quickly and acted before really thinking? He had made a huge mistake, and he was trying to atone for it. Looking at Conner breathing so peacefully, he wanted to walk over, touch him gently and say, "Forget Carmine and let's ride back to Montana and concentrate on finding Deanna. She is the one who offers you what you are really looking for."

Still, Dudley knew more about Deanna than he was revealing. She was a mystery woman that had been popping in and out of every place between Dry Gulch and Fairview for years. She, in her own way, was a legend as men and women alike, for years, had been captivated with her beauty, mysterious ways and air of sophistication.

Dudley at this point rose with a quickening pulse. Suppose he, alone, entered that house by stealth, like a burglar and surveyed the scene for clues. He brushed the idea away. Still, he needed information, so he discounted the danger and moved forward with a plan.

THE GIRL WHO RODE INTO A STORM

He turned away from the window, turned back to it and looked once more at the tall front of the building opposite his room; then, he started to get ready for the expedition. He put on the grey pants and shirt he had, assuming they would make him less detectible in the dark. Since it might be necessary to remain as invisible as possible, he obscured the last bit of white that showed in his outfit with a black neck scarf. He checked out his revolver to make sure it was loaded. His fingers went deftly over it, fondling it like a lover. It was his protection and it had gotten him out of many jams over the years.

He then went outside and strolled down the street, passing the house opposite, with a close scrutiny. A narrow, paved sidewalk ran between it and the house on its right, and all the windows opening on this small court were dark. Moreover, the house which was his quarry was set back several feet from the street, an indentation which would completely hide him from anyone who looked from the street. He went to the end of the block, crossed over and, turning back on the far side of the street, slipped into the opening between the houses. Instantly he was in dense darkness. For four stories above him the two buildings towered, shutting out the starlight. Looking straight up he found only a faint reflection of the glow of the city lights in the sky.

He saw a cellar window. He tried it and found it locked, but a little manoeuvring with his knife enabled him to turn the catch at the top of the lower sash. Then he raised it slowly and leaned into the blackness. Something incredibly soft, tenuous, clinging, pressed at once against his face. He started back with a shudder and brushed away the remnants of a big spider web. Then he leaned into an intense blackness. He slipped through the opening at once, and beneath his feet there was a soft crunching of coal. He had come directly into the bin. Turning, he closed the window, as he did not want to alert anyone who might be strolling outside and notice the open window.

As he stood surrounded by hostile silence, he grew accustomed to the dimness, and he could make out, not definite objects, but faint, indistinct outlines. Presently he took out a match, struck it and examined his surroundings. He stepped out of the coal bin and noticed several dilapidated chairs and cabinets piled together in a tangled mass. He looked at them with a shudder, as if he read in them the history of the ruin, fall and death of many an old inhabitant of the house. It seemed to his excited imagination that the man with the sneer had been the cause of much of the destruction and would be the cause of more. There was evil lurking about within this house.

He reached the stairs and ascended slowly. Halfway up, the door above him suddenly opened and light poured down. He saw the flying figure of a cat, a broom behind it and a woman behind the broom. "Outta here you nasty thing," she shouted.

The cat brushed Dudley's knee, screeched and disappeared below; the woman with the broom shaded her eyes and peered down the steps. He leaned to his left against the wall and fortunately the match had gone out when the door was opened and a gust of wind came down. Apparently she did not see him.

He eased up to the top of the stairs but the door was latched from the other side. He paused a moment to consider how he was going to get in, but, while he stayed there contemplating, he heard the rattle of pots and pans. Apparently she was washing the cooking utensils, and that meant she was probably near the close of her work for the evening. In fact, the rim of light, which showed between the door frame and the door, suddenly snapped out, and he heard her footsteps retreating. Still he delayed a moment or two, for fear she might return to take something which she had forgotten. But the silence deepened above him, and voices were faintly audible toward the front of the house.

He pulled out his pocket knife and adroitly slid it between the door and the jam, easily lifting the latch up and off. He opened the door, thankful for the well-oiled hinges which kept it from making any noise, and fortunately there was a shaft of light coming in the windows from the full moon. He observed a door to his right, opening into the main part of the house. He passed through the doorway and sighed with relief when his foot touched the carpet on the hall beyond. He noted, too, that there was no sign of a creak from the boards beneath his tread.

THE GIRL WHO RODE INTO A STORM

He slipped down the shadow of the main stairs, swiftly circled through the danger of the light of the lower hall lamp and started his ascent. The thick carpet muffled every sound which he made in climbing. He reached the second floor hallway. This, beyond doubt, was where he would find the room of the woman who was causing so much consternation. He opened the first door to his left. It was a small linen closet. Determining to be methodical, he went to the extreme end of the hall and tried that door. It was locked, but, while his hand was still on the knob, turning it in disappointment, a door, higher up in the house, opened and a hum of voices passed out to him. They grew louder; they turned to the staircase from the floor above and commenced to descend at a running pace. By the pounding sound, it was evidently men, perhaps three or four of them. He started for the dark corner at the end of the hallway and hid in the darkness.

As the men were leaving, a woman came down the stairs. It must be Carmine Jones he thought. She was at the top of the landing and as she stepped onto the first step of the stairs, Dudley leapt out and grabbed her, whispering into her right ear as he cupped his hands over her mouth, "Scream and I'll have to hurt you."

Totally unafraid, pointing at a door down the hall she said, "In there, so we can talk."

She led the way a few steps down the hall, and he followed her through the door, working his mind frantically in an effort to find words with

J. WAYNE FRYE

which to open his speech. He saw a dressing table, an Empire bed covered with green-figured silk, a pleasant rug on the floor, and, just as he had gathered an impression of delightful femininity from these furnishings, the girl turned on the Tiffany lamp on the dressing table, and he saw not Carmine Jones, but a bronze-haired beauty, as different from Conner's love interest as day is from night.

He was conscious then only of beautiful green-blue eyes, very wide, very bright, and lips that parted on a word and froze there in silence. "You're not…"

"I am not who?" asked the girl with amazing steadiness. But he saw her hand go back to the dressing table and open, with incredible deftness and speed, the little top drawer behind her. "Don't do that!" said Dudley softly, but sharply. "Keep your hand off that table, lady, if you know what's good for you. Stand away from it please," he said, as he pointed to a chair. "Take a seat."

She hesitated. In that moment she seemed to see that he was earnest, and that it would be foolish to tamper with him. So, she obeyed without a word. Her eyes, to be sure, flickered here and there about the room, as though they sought some means of sending a warning to her friends, or finding some escape for herself. Then her glance returned to Dudley as she settled into a chair. She thought to herself that Dudley did not seem a very sinister looking fellow, but there was something deadly about his eyes. They were a soft, dark brown but there was a definite sincerity in them, a sincerity that said, "I mean business."

The girl's face hardened strangely. "What your game is I don't know, but I'll tell you this: I'm letting you play as if you had all the cards in the deck. But you haven't. I've got one ace that'll take all your trumps. Suppose I scream out. You'd be done for."

"You won't," he said.

She looked him squarely, with determination, in the eyes. "Don't dare me. I hate a dare worse than anything in the world, almost," she said as her green-blue eyes were pools of light flashing angrily at him.

Into the right hand of Dudley, with magic speed and skilful grace came the long, glimmering body of his revolver, and, holding it at his hip, he levelled it at her as he said, "If you scream, it will be the last sound you ever make."

She shrank back at that, gasping. For there was an utter surety about Dudley's handling of the weapon. His high pitched voice and effeminate manner had thrown her off, but the heavy gun balanced and steadied in his slim fingers, as if it were no more than a feather's weight, made the woman realize this person meant business.

Still, she was not completely obedient, as she said, "You're bluffing. I'm going through that door!" Straight for the door she went.

"Go back!" he commanded. He swiftly moved to the door and blocked her way, but the gun hung futile in his hand as she stared at him.

THE GIRL WHO RODE INTO A STORM

"It's easy to pull a gun," said the girl, with something of a sneer, "but it takes nerve to use it."

If half a dozen men had poured through the doorway, Dudley would have felt no fear and pulled the trigger with no remorse. But this one girl was enough to make him helpless. He looked at her in amazement. She had not gone; in fact, she had defiantly stood with her back against the door, staring at him in speechless bewilderment and stoic determination.

"What sort of a man are you, anyway?" asked the girl.

"Not much of one, apparently, based upon my present actions. I probably never have been, but I shot a guy a few days ago, and have lived to regret it. He was the only man I ever shot in my life. Go out and round up your friends; I can't stop you. At heart, I am a coward I guess as my talk is bolder than my actions. I hate violence and have used bravado to intimidate people," and then he smiled and continued, "but I always knew I could not follow through. You sensed that, which is why you bested me. My hats off to you."

"Listen to me," she said suddenly. "I have two minutes to talk to you, and I'll give you those two minutes. You can use them in getting out of the house. I'll show you a way, or you can use them to tell me just why you've come."

Dudley smiled. "Lady," he said, "if a rat was in a trap do you think he would stop very long between a chance of getting clear and a chance to tell how he come to get into the place?"

"I have a perfectly good reason for asking," she answered. "Even if you now get out of the house safely you'll try to come back later on."

"Do I look like that big a fool?"

She seemed to be giving his question some thought as she said, "You are not like any other man I have ever seen. Frankly, I sized you up as a bit of a sissy, but I have to admit when you pulled that gun I was scared. My guess is you'll come back, because I see an intensity of purpose. You are not the kind of person to give up easily. And this is all about Carmine Jones isn't it?"

"Yes."

"You don't have to talk to me," said the girl. "As a matter of fact I shouldn't be here listening to you. I don't know why, but I want to help you. I am, for some reason, sympathetic toward you. You in love with Carmine?"

"No."

Her expression grew grave and cold again. "Then why are you here hunting for her? What do you want with her?"

"Lady," said Dudley, "I will put all my cards on the table. I am looking for Carmine, yes, but I also am trying to find out the story behind a man who appears in the window looking out at her, and apparently giving her directions to avoid my friend who does have feelings for her. He seems sinister. I don't know what he is. I don't know what you are, but I figure that you and Carmine and everybody else in this house are under the malevolent influence of that man."

Her eyes darkened with a shadow of alarm. "Go on."

"I'm guessing about what you all are and what you are up to. All I know is what I'm here trying to do. I'm not working for myself. I'm working for a friend I care about very deeply who is fascinated by Carmine."

She said, "That's the man who stopped her on the street today?"

"Yes. He started after her, not even knowing her real name, with just an image of her. We found out that she lived in sight of the river in Denver, and pretty soon we located her here."

"And what are you hoping to do?"

"To find her and talk to her without her suffering undue influence from whomever it was looking out the window at her from this house. It is obvious she is afraid of him."

"Can't he find her and tell her those things for himself?"

"He tried to, but that fellow in the window was obviously exerting influence on her."

"And suppose she is influenced by this sinister man, what are you going to do about it. You don't seem very capable, based upon what I see, of doing any real harm to someone."

"Lady, I know what I might appear to be, but believe me, in a pinch, I am a guy you can rely on, a guy who never backs down from a fight. Just because I didn't use a gun on a woman doesn't mean I am not capable of using one."

"You just backed down with me."

"Have I really backed down? Or, did I just decide that you weren't all that bad, and that I didn't want to hurt you?"

"I've one thing to tell you," she said, breaking in swiftly on him. "Do what you want and take all the chances you want, but, if you value your life and the life of your friend, keep away from the man you saw in the window, and I warn you if he gives you a slow, sinister grin be ready to suffer dire consequences. That is when you will have no chance at all. The moment he knows your hand is against him, I don't care how brave or how clever you are, you're doomed!"

She spoke with such a passion and grim conviction with her voice quivering and her eyes growing wide, that there seemed to be a rising breath of cold wind swirling into the room.

"Don't you see," she went on gently, "that I am trying to help someone who I see as well-intentioned, but naive? It's the first and the last time that I'm going to see you, so I can talk. I know you're honest in your convictions, and I know you have a good heart. I can see the depth of your whole character in the way you've stood by your friend; and, if there's a possible way of helping you, I'll do it. But you must promise me first that you'll never cross the man you saw in the window."

"I don't think I could promise that. There's a chill in my body now in regards to him that tells me I'm going to meet up with him and something bad is going to happen."

She gasped at that revelation, and, stepping back from him, she appeared to be searching her mind to discover something which would finally and completely convince him of the folly involved in confronting the man. At length she found it.

"Do I look to you like a coward?" she said. "Do I seem to be weak in mind, body or spirit?"

Looking at her with conviction, Dudley replied, "No, definitely not."

"And what will a woman fight hardest for?"

"For her children." said Dudley after a moment of thought. "And, to be with the man she loves - to ultimately marry that man."

A look of determination creased her pursing lips as she said, "Or, to accept her fate and marry a man she doesn't love."

"Yes," said Dudley. "But these are modern times; a woman can't be forced to marry against her will."

"I am going to marry the man you saw in the window," she said simple and direct as she, with dull, patient eyes watched Dudley's soft, wrinkle free face develop deep furrows and grow pale, as if a he had seen a ghost.

"You, marry that abominable creature?"

"Yes," she whispered.

"You couldn't love that man. Nobody could love that man. I can tell when you speak of him that you have intense dislike of him. That you fear him."

"I, I don't know" she stammered. "He's actually kind sometimes."

THE GIRL WHO RODE INTO A STORM

"No, I can sense your distaste for him. You hate him," insisted Dudley. "And he is to have you, that despicable man?" He moved a little to her side, as she turned toward him, smiling faintly and allowing the light to come more clearly and fully on her face. "You are meant for better, lady; you have good in you. I can see it. I can sense it. I can literally feel it. When you find the right man you can love, why lady, he'll be privileged to call you his wife, not because of your incredible beauty, but because you have a good heart. I can sense it. I am good at sensing those things, because the truth is I am kind hearted too, despite my occasional fits of temper and impetuousness."

The ghost of a flush bloomed in her cheeks, but her faint smile did not falter, and she seemed to be hearing him from far away. "The man you saw in the window," she said with conviction, "will never talk to me like that, and still I shall marry him."

"Tell me your name," asked Dudley.

"Rena Tilson."

"Listen to me, Rena. Don't do this to yourself. That man is evil. I can tell it."

She shook her head, as her eyes seemed to moisten over. She glared at him, but could find no words. Dudley, his bronzed soft skin glimmering in the moonlight filtering through the window to their right, said, "If I've taken this perilous journey from Dry Gulch to here and stuck my head in a trap, as you might say, for the sake of a man I only recently met, but who is the finest, gentleman I have ever known, don't you think I

J. WAYNE FRYE

would stick my neck out to prevent a woman like you from a life of misery with that cretin?"

"You are sticking your nose into something that is absolutely, without a doubt, none of your business," she replied.

"You know Rena. You may be right. I have befriended a man who has stirred something in me. I should have butted out of his business and never taken up his cause. Yet, here I am for some reason. I cannot see him in misery. It has such an adverse effect on me, makes me feel that I must try and make his life better. I know I caused a lot of his misery through impetuous actions, and I want to, more than anything else in the world, for some unknown reason, help him find love in his life."

Rena said, "You have an unhealthy obsession with this man. It isn't normal."

"Rena," Dudley, with softness in his voice, replied, "I am not normal as defined by a society run by a pack of hypocrites always pointing fingers of condemnation. I am a person who will not tolerate disrespect, and people know that about me, and that is why they give me a wide berth after they get acquainted with me, because they know I am not a person with whom you trifle. I am here to tell you that what you are submitting to in marrying this man is disrespect for yourself. When I see a girl who gets past being just pretty and starts in being beautiful, which you are, I cannot understand how you could demean yourself in such a way."

The far away look in her moistened eyes came back. She was looking at Dudley now with a sort of sad wonder. "Do you know what I am?" she said gravely.

"Let me tell you something. I do not know or care. I can see the real you. I have heard of a woman named Deanna Defoe. She is a free spirited woman who occasionally pops up all over lower Montana along the rail line between Fairview and Dry Gulch. She is a woman who can be brazen in her demeanour, but she carries herself with pride, and the few men who have known her intimately have never forgotten the encounters I am sure, because she has no shame for being a woman, and she tolerates no disrespect. I sense you are the same type woman."

Bowing her head, and then raising it and looking into Dudley's eyes, she said, "I have heard of her too, and her extraordinary beauty. She is a legend of sorts with her uncanny ability at cards, but above all, I have heard of her beauty and the piercing, dancing, deep set dark eyes that seem to mesmerize men and bring them to their knees in adoration of this will-o-the-wisp woman who seems to dart in and out of one place after another, always disappearing almost into thin air. She is a woman to be admired, and I am sure that she would not allow any man to subjugate her."

"No, but I sense from what I hear that she is a lonely sort, always on the move, never able to grasp the reality of a steady relationship with a man who can accept her uniqueness."

"I know loneliness, Dudley. I'm touched by what you say, but I must marry this man." She sighed and continued. "I'm going down to see that man, and I'm going to tell him that Bob Morgan, whom I am to tell to see him is not in his room, that he didn't answer my knock, and then that I looked around through the house and didn't find him. After that I'm coming back here, and I'm going to try to get an opportunity for you to talk to Carmine Jones." She sighed deeply and one could see sincerity in her eyes as she continued. "It isn't for your friend who is asleep, but it's to give you a chance to finish this business and come to the end of this trail and go back to your home, free of curiosity and doubt. Because, if you stay around here long, there'll be trouble, a lot of trouble, and I hate to see you hurt. Now stay here and wait for me. If anyone taps at the door, you'd better slip into that closet in the corner. Will you wait?"

"Yes."

"You trust me?"

"I may be foolish, but yes, I am going to trust you."

She smiled at him with conviction and was gone, as a foreboding hush fell over the house and a quiet that was actually so loud it felt deafening. He went to the window and looked down to the lonely street bathed in the darkness of lost hope. It seemed impossible that he had gotten himself so entangled in mystery just because of a temper tantrum over the belief a man named Conner had stolen his horse.

Suddenly, from somewhere in the house the muffled sound of mayhem rose. Dudley ran to the door, thinking of Rena. Then, a door squeaked loudly as it was opened and the voice of a man shouted, "Help, help!"

Other voices answered far away, and someone said, "Someone is in the house. The window in the cellar was tampered with. I saw knife marks on it when I went to the coal bin."

Dudley stepped back close to the door of the closet and waited. It would mean a search was imminent. And a search was quickly instituted as one man shouted instructions, and the last instruction was chilling, "Don't ask questions, when you see someone you don't know, shoot on sight and shoot to kill."

Dudley heard them approach the door of the room, and he slipped into the closet. At once a cloud of soft, cool silks brushed about him, and he worked his way backward until his shoulders had touched the wall at the back of the closet. Luckily the enclosure was deep, and the clothes were hanging thickly from the racks. It was sufficient to conceal him from any careless searcher, but it would do no good if anyone probed; and certainly these men were not ones to search carelessly. Strangely, he found himself stroking the nice silk dresses and frilly blouses. For some reason, they gave him comfort.

He was on the verge of slipping out and making a mad break for the door of the house and trying to escape by taking the men by surprise, when he heard the door of the room open and someone, no not just someone, Rena said, "No need for worry. It is just a burglar who knows nothing."

Dudley felt reassured by the calm in her voice, but perhaps it was what he could not see that betrayed her, as the man with her said, "What's wrong? You're acting nervous."

"Isn't there reason enough to make me nervous?" she asked. "A robber is at large in the house."

The man was having none of it. "Devilish queer the way you are acting. There's something wrong. What is it?"

There was no answer. Then the voice began again, soft and gentle. "In the old days you used to keep nothing from me; we were companions. That was when you were a child. Now that you are a woman, when you feel more, think more, see more, when our companionship should be like a running stream, continually bringing new things into life, I find barriers between us. Why is it, my dear?"

Still there was no answer. Dudley's pulse began to quicken, as though the question had been asked of him, as though he himself were fumbling for the answer. He was still fondling the silk clothing for comfort.

"Talk to me, Rena," said the man. "Try to open your mind to me. There are things which you dislike in me; I know it. Just what those things are I cannot tell, but we must break down these foolish little barriers which are appearing more and more every day. Not that I mean to intrude myself on every moment of your life. You understand that, of course?"

"Of course," said Rena faintly.

"And I understand perfectly that you have passed out of childhood into young womanhood, and that is a dreamy time for a girl. Her body is formed at last, but her mind is only half formed. There is a pleasant mist over it. Very well, I don't wish to brush the mist away. If I did that I would take half that charm away from you. No, I shall always let you live your own life. All that I ask for, my dear, are certain commitments. Let us establish them before it is too late, or you will find one day that you have married an old man, and we shall have silent dinners. There is nothing more wretched than that. If it should come about, then you will begin to look on me as a jailer, and I would not want that."

Suddenly, Dudley felt a tinge of sympathy with the man who obviously must have genuine feelings for Rena, as he said tenderly, "You are shrinking from me, because you feel that I am too old for you."

"No, that is not true," she said as a hand pounded heavily on the door.

"The idiots have found something," said the man and he shouted, "Come in."

Then, Dudley heard a panting voice a moment later exclaim, "We've got him!"

Chapter 7
With Anger in His Heart

Dudley put his hand on his gun, preparing for any eventuality as the man who came in said, "It was down in the cellar that we found the first tracks. He came in through the side window. He dropped into the coal dust and left prints. He obviously is an amateur as he didn't have the sense to wipe them off."

"You followed his trail, then" said the sinister sounding older man.

"Up the stairs to the kitchen and down the hall and up to Harry's room, but he left that room again and came down the hall. The coal dust was pretty well wiped off by that time, but we held a light close to the carpet and got the signs of it."

"And where did it lead?" asked the older man.

"Right to this room!"

Dudley stepped from among the smooth silks and pressed close to the door of the closet, his hand on the knob. The time had almost come for one desperate attempt to escape, and he was ready to bolt out with gun in hand.

A moment of pause had come, a pause which, in the imagination of Dudley, was filled with the unbearable apprehension as the older man said, "Nope, not possible."

"I can show you the tracks."

The older man, impatient now, said, "You fool, they simply grew dim when they got to this door. I've been here for some time. Go back and tell them to hunt some more. Go up to the attic and search there. That's the place an amateur would most likely hide."

The man growled some retort and left, closing the door heavily behind him as the older man said, "Now Rena, tell me the truth."

Apprehension grew within Dudley. Had the man guessed at the truth? Had he sent his follower away, merely to avoid having it known that a man had taken shelter in the room of the girl he loved? "Go on," the older man repeated. "Let me hear the whole truth."

"I-I-I, stammered the girl and she could say no more.

The man laughed unpleasantly. "Let me help you. It was somebody you met somewhere on the train, perhaps, and you couldn't help smiling at him, right? You smiled so much, in fact, that he followed you and found that you had come here. The only way he could get in was by stealth. Is that right? So he came in exactly that way, like a robber, but really only to keep a tryst with you? A pretty story, a true romance. I begin to see why you find me such a dull fellow, my dear girl."

"John," began Rena, her voice shaking.

He broke in as smoothly as ever. "Let me tell the story for you and spare your blushes. This fellow is all worked up over you. He was in here and you told him to get out the window before I came in."

"Yes," said Rena.

Then John moved toward the closet as he said, "Liar."

Before he got to the door, Dudley pushed it open and stepped into the room, gun in hand. The man was shocked by the sight of the Colt levelled at him. Rena did not cry out, but every muscle in her face and body seemed to contract, as if she were preparing herself for the explosion.

"You don't have to put up your hands," said Dudley, wondering at the familiarity of the face of the man. He had brooded on it so often in the past few days that it was like the face of an old acquaintance. He knew every line in that sharp profile from when he saw him in the window.

"Thank you," responded John, and, turning to Rena, he said coldly in a sardonic, sarcastic manner. "I congratulate you on your glorious taste," as he fought back laughter. "This dandy is a real Adonis." He then shook his head and laughed out loud. "What a prissy peacock of a man."

He turned back to Dudley. "And I suppose you have overhead our entire conversation?"

"Of course."

"Will you be staying in Denver long?"

"I don't know yet. It depends on a lot of things."

"Meaning that I'm liable to put an end to your stay?"

"Maybe!"

"I suppose Rena has filled your head with a lot of rot about what a terrible fellow I am, but I am sure, as you can now see, I am a very quiet and ordinary kind of person."

"None of that matters right now. Just oblige me, please," Dudley replied in his soft voice. "Just stand right where you are."

"Are you capable of murder?"

"When a person is cornered, he is capable of a lot of things."

"You are the man with the gun, so that gives you the upper hand." He turned toward Rena. "I see that your dandy here is a most determined knight in shining armour. I suppose he'll instantly abduct you and sweep you away before my eyes? Go right ahead. By the way, my name is John Markham."

Nonchalantly, Dudley said, "Please to make your acquaintance. I am Dudley Danforth."

Sneering, John said, "Dudley, name certainly fits you. Now tell me the story of why you came to this house, the real story, because I know it was not just to see a girl. You don't look like the kind of man interested in a girl."

"Your smugness is not appreciated, nor your derogatory evaluation of me. I came to see a girl, and her name is Carmine Jones."

Relief, wonder, and even a gleam of outright happiness shot into the eyes of John Markham. "You came for that?" Suddenly he laughed heartily, but it seemed somehow tinged with emotion, as he continued. "Now, what about Carmine?"

"I want to see her. I expect that you will send for her and tell her that she is free to go down with me, leave this house for an unobserved talk with my friend."

"A bit pushy I think. Why not talk to her here?"

"I sense that she is under some kind of restraint here."

His demeanour was more hostile, as he said, "No doubt, you expect to take her to meet Conner McCord."

"You know him then?"

A smirk grew on his face. "I am familiar with the young man's name, yes."

"Well, you are right. I intend to let her speak to him without your prying eyes observing."

"And why should I accede to that request? Carmine Jones might be a person of great value to me whom I do not want to let out of my sight for very good reasons."

"Well, I have some very good reasons why she should speak to Mr. McCord unencumbered by your watchfulness. It is pretty obvious she is frightened of you, very fearful."

"I don't believe you have a very solid case for me letting her leave with you."

Dudley slowly, with determination, pointed the gun, the great equalizer among men, and smiled. "This says I do."

Absolutely showing no fear whatsoever, John Markham said, "Go out of this house with a dandy dude like you, a veritable abomination of all that is manly. I send for the girl; I request her to go down with you to the street and take a walk, because you wish to talk to her. Heavens man, I can't persuade her to go with a stranger at night, to walk out with a prancing peacock of disgusting contradictions. Surely you see that!"

"I'll persuade her, if given the chance."

"And, when you're on the streets with the girl, do you suppose I'll rest idle and let you walk away with her?"

"Once we are outside the house, it's your call Mr. Markham, but I will be out in the open, and I think your common sense will make you exercise restraint. If you act foolish though, I wear a gun for a reason. Not that I figure on bragging, but I want you to pick good men for my tail and tell them to tread lightly with me, because my appearance may say one thing, but my intentions can turn as deadly as a rattle snake in the noon-day sun."

"Aside from certain idiosyncrasies, such as your manner of paying a call by way of a cellar window, I think you are a person of honour. Now, I like to think so am I."

THE GIRL WHO RODE INTO A STORM

Impressed with Markham's articulation prowess, and apparent respect for honourable people, Dudley said, "Suppose we shake hands to bind the bargain? You send for Carmine Jones, and I will try to persuade her to leave with me. If she agrees, when we are safe to the doors of the house; the minute we step into the street, you are free to do anything you want to get either of us. Will you shake on that?"

There was some hesitation on Markham's part, but within a couple of seconds he extended his hand to Dudley. There was power in his grip as he clasp Dudley's soft, puffy hand and pumped it up and down.

A great rage suddenly appeared in Markham's eyes, as if there had been a fire lit within his belly and it was burning with intensity. He eased into a nearby chair, containing his rage out of common sense that the person before him had a gun in his hand which gave him a distinct advantage, despite his seemingly effeminate ways.

"I have no doubt, in a fair fight, I could best you Mr. Danforth, but we have shaken hands, and I am a man who values a handshake, no matter whose hand I shake, be it a priest, a banker, a pauper or a dandy like you.

Dudley could see a flash of resentment detailed in Markham's scowl, but he had accepted the agreement and, for some reason, Dudley felt that he should honour that agreement. He did not fully trust him, but, for the time being, he was going to give him the benefit of the doubt.

THE GIRL WHO RODE INTO A STORM

"Very well then Mr. Danforth, I'll send for Carmine Jones, but you'll never get her away from this house without force."

A servant answered the bell almost at once. "Tell Carmine she's wanted in Miss Tilson's room," said Markham, and, when the servant disappeared, he began pacing up and down the room. Now and then he cast a sharp glance to the side and scrutinized Dudley. He paused in his pacing and looked directly at Rena, and, with his feet spread and his head bowed in an absurd Napoleonic posture, he considered every feature of her face. The uncertain discomfort, which came trembling on her face, elicited no response from him.

It was obvious to Dudley that she feared him. Still one could sense that she had a certain affection for him, partly as the result of many benefactions, no doubt, and partly from long acquaintance; and, above all, she respected his powers of mind intensely. The play of emotion in her face - fear, anger, suspicion – was obvious.

With satisfaction, Dudley saw that her glances continually sought him, timidly and curiously. All vanity aside, he had dropped a bomb on Markham, and he could sense that he was a slow burning fuse that could make that bomb explode. The question was when?

There was a tap at the door. It opened and Carmine Jones entered in a dressing gown. She smiled brightly at Rena and mildly at Markham, then musingly at Dudley.

J. WAYNE FRYE

THE GIRL WHO RODE INTO A STORM

"This dandy excuse of a man" said a sarcastic Markham, "is Dudley Danforth."

Dudley nodded his head in recognition, while ignoring Markham's contemptuous remark, as he continued, "He has come to persuade you to go out for a stroll with him, so that he can talk to you about that curious fellow, Conner McCord. He is going to try to soften your heart, I believe, by telling you all the inconveniences which the fellow has endured to find you here. But he will do his talking for himself. Just why he has to take you out of the house, at night, before he can talk to you is, I admit, a mystery to me. But let him do the persuading."

Dudley turned to his host, a cold gleam in his eyes. His case had been presented in such a way as to make his task of persuasion almost impossible. Then he turned back and looked at Carmine. Her face was a little pale, he thought, but perfectly composed.

"I don't know Conner McCord," she said. "Of course, I'm glad to talk to you, Mr. Danforth, but why not here?"

Markham covered a smile of satisfaction, and the girl looked at him, apparently to see if she had spoken correctly. It was obvious that the leader was pleased, and she glanced back at Dudley, with a flush of subdued pleasure.

Dudley, with deep conviction in his voice said, "I can't talk to you here for what I believe is coercion, because, while you're under the same roof with this man," and then he turned and stared at Markham, "you live in fear of him, being so frightened that you cannot speak and think freely under his roof. You feel him around you and behind you and beside you every minute, and you keep wondering not what you really feel about anything, but what John Markham wants you to feel."

She glanced apprehensively at Markham, and, seeing that he did not move to resent this assertion, she looked again with wide-eyed wonder at Dudley.

"You see," said Markham to Carmine Jones, "our friend from Montana has a child-like faith in my apparent hypnotic power over you."

A faint smile of agreement flickered on her lips and went out. Then, she regarded Dudley with an utter lack of emotion.

Looking directly into Carmine's eyes, Dudley said, "He is a smooth talker, smother than I am apparently, but I know if I could get you out of this house that you might level with me, tell me the truth about why you wanted to meet Conner McCord, but now claim to never have heard of him. We are both worried about you seeming to be a captive here. As far as going out with me is concerned, all I can do is ask you to look at me close, and then ask yourself if I'm the sort of person a girl should be afraid of. I won't keep you long; five minutes is all I ask. And we can walk up and down the street, in plain view of the house, if you want. I just want you to know that Conner and I are interested in your welfare."

THE GIRL WHO RODE INTO A STORM

At least he had broken through the surface of indifference previously displayed by Carmine as she was looking at him now, with a shade of interest and sympathy, but she shook her head very slow left to right indicating she was not going with him.

"I am afraid," she whispered sheepishly.

"Think about it Carmine. Conner and I have worked pretty hard to find you. I broke into this house tonight, risking arrest, and maybe even death just to talk with you. I frankly have asked myself why I am taking this risk for a man I only met a few days ago, but Conner is truly one of the finest men I have ever known. He has stirred something in me like no one else ever has. He may be a bit childlike in so many ways, but he has a certain quality about him that makes me want to care for him, protect him, make sure he is not harmed in any way physically, emotionally or psychologically," he said as the look on his face reflected deep sincerity.

Markham, Rena and Carmine all were surprised by what Dudley had said. His affection for Conner bordered on that which they dared not breech in polite conversation at a time in America, much like today, when voicing affection for someone of the same sex was considered an approbation of propriety. The world then in America, like today, was one where religion was used to condemn and ridicule rather than to absolve and compliment. Condemnation feels good for hypocrites and it is and was then a tenet of religion and politics that never supports progression, but embraces the status-quo where prejudice and lack of compassion is somehow promoted as embracing sanctity. The three there with Dudley that night were all victims and did not even know it. They were victims of a nation where conformity was the norm in a society that shouted how democratic it was, but had no tolerance for anyone who challenged conventionality. Dudley realized what they were thinking, and he took a deep breath, as he realized he may have gone too far and lost his edge.

"Look," said Dudley, "I may have gone a bit far in my remarks about how I feel about Conner, but that does not belie the fact that I am here to see if I can help him to somehow, dear Carmine, reach out to you and either elevate the relationship he seeks or to allow him to see that it has no hope to ever bring fruit to the tree of hope he has planted in his mind. Just give me a chance to talk to you. That is all I ask."

It was obvious that she was contemplating. It was curious to her that this effeminate looking fellow had come as an emissary from Conner McCord. Dudley's devotion to his friend was admirable. She turned to Rena and said, "What shall I do?"

Rena Tilson glanced apprehensively at John Markham and then flushed, but she raised her head bravely. "If I were you, Carmine," she said with conviction, "I'd simply ask myself if I could trust this man. Can you?"

Carmine turned to Dudley again, with a look of indecisiveness. Certainly, she thought, if sincerity was ever written on the face of someone, it was obvious in Dudley.

"Yes," she said, "I'll go, but only for a few minutes and in the street right in front of the house."

John Markham was not pleased. He rose and glided across the room, as if to go elsewhere and vent his anger alone. "Touché, Mr. Danforth." Then he turned toward Carmine, "A man more violent than I would not allow this; would physically restrain you Carmine. You remember, that woman, when he's talking to you. I want you constantly to remember that."

"Wait!" cut in Dudley sharply. "She'll do her own thinking, without your help."

John Markham bowed with a sardonic smile, but his face was colourless. Plainly he had been hard hit by the turn of events. "Later on," he said with blazing eyes aimed at Dudley, "we'll see more of each other, and it might not be a pleasant meeting."

Dudley replied, "I will look forward to it."

"Don't count on it being a meeting you will embrace gladly."

Dudley made his way toward the door where Markham stood, and said to Carmine, "I'll wait for you to get dressed. I'll be in front of the house. Wait, no I won't. I'll wait by the front door to be sure no effort is made to prevent you from joining me."

Carmine Jones nodded, flung one frightened and appealing glance to Rena for direction and then hurried out to her room to dress. Dudley turned back to Rena. He smiled at her and said as Markham moved to the doorway, "Thanks. You are a very fair minded lady and I do mean lady. Your help is appreciated."

He turned, hesitated a bit and walked past Markham toward the front door as Markham said to him, "There is steel in you, the kind of steel I wouldn't expect in someone who looks like you do. We are going to have a confrontation one day, and it will be sooner than you think."

"Looking forward to it," said Dudley, as the two heard the swift pattering of feet on the stairs. Presently, Carmine was moving very slowly toward him down the hall. Plainly she was bitterly afraid when she came beside him, under the dim hall light. She wore a black hat, turned slightly down over her forehead. She indicated a faint show of doubt, when Dudley squelched it by escorting her down the stairs and quickly opening the front door and, stepping out into the starlight, inviting her with a smile and a gesture to follow. In a moment they were in the freshness of the night air. He took her slender arm, and they passed slowly down the stoop steps. At the bottom she turned and looked anxiously back at the house.

"Lady," murmured Dudley, "there's nothing to be afraid of. We're going to walk right up and down this street and never get out of sight of the people in that infernal house." He, holding her arm, felt her shiver quietly, as he continued, "Unless, of course, you want to go farther of your own free will."

"No, no!" she exclaimed, as if frightened by the very prospect.

"Then we won't. It's all up to you. You're the one in control."

"But tell me what you want quickly, please," she urged. "I need to get right back."

"O.K., I'll get right down to it. Conner McCord simply told me about the correspondence between the two of you, and how you let him know you were coming through Dry Gulch and wanted to see him."

"I don't understand," quizzically replied the girl

"Well, you should understand that Conner has a hole in his heart, a hole left by you. Don't get me wrong, he has actually had a few dalliances with another woman, but this is a woman he will never have, and he knows it. It is a woman so unusual that she has only motivated his desire even more to court you. He sees in you something special, something that gnaws at his insides, something that you raised up deep within him with your correspondence, but then you let flounder in a sea of doubt."

She was moved now, and no longer was going to deny Conner. She tilted her head down and one could sense her emotions boiling to the surface. She was struggling to continue being the uncaring, denying woman who had turned him aside so assiduously with a prompt dismissal.

"The whole thing was only a joke. I didn't really mean to…" she said, unable to finish.

"Do you know what that joke did?" asked Dudley. "It made two men fight, then forge a friendship together and get on the trail of a girl whose name they didn't even know. They found the girl, and then she said she had forgotten the emotions she had stirred in this man. There is something sinister behind it all. But I want to explain one thing. The reason that Conner didn't get to that train wasn't because he didn't try. He did try. He tried so hard that he got into a fight with a temperamental person who tried to hold him up for a desperate measure he took to get to you in Dry Gulch, and Conner was shot by this fool, shot and made to miss the connection with you."

"Shot?" asked the girl. "Shot?"

Suddenly she was clutching his arm tightly, terrified at the thought of Conner being shot. She recovered herself at once and drew away, eluding the hand of Dudley. But he had lifted the mask of emotion deep within her and saw the real state of her mind; and she, too, knew that the secret was discovered. It angered her that she had let her guard down.

"I tell you what I guessed from the window," said Dudley. "You went down to the street, all prepared to meet up with poor old Conner, but there was someone who warned you against any connection, someone who somehow knew we were in town, someone who for a reason I am not privy to, wanted you not to spend any time with Conner McCord."

"What could anyone be afraid of in that house?" she said as she looked back at it.

"Afraid of you leaving."

This seemed to arouse fear in her as she said, "What do you know?"

"I know this," he answered, "that I think a girl like you is very special. Any woman who could attract a man like Conner has to be special."

"So, he sends another man to risk his life to find me and tell me about it?" she stated with obvious anger and sadness both.

"He didn't send me. I just came of my own accord. He has given up inside and his heart is wilting with pain that he has been rejected by you. (He did not share with her that it was two women's rejection that was causing the pain.) But the reason I came was because I care about Conner, never cared about anybody more in my life. He is a special man."

"I detest a man who won't fight for the woman he loves," said Carmine.

"It's because he figures he is not worthy of you and figures he has lost any chance with you. Besides, he can't talk about himself. He's no good at that. But, if it comes to fighting lady, why he rode a horse nearly to death and stole another and had a gunfight, all for the sake of seeing you when that train passed through Dry Gulch. I thought I would do what I could for such a fine man and tell you his feelings for you, feelings that I can understand, because I love someone too, but I have no one to speak for me, and I know that I will never see my love come to fruition, because of a world where all the cards are stacked against me, but I want to see my friend Conner realize his dream of having a relationship with a woman of character. You could never do any better than Conner McCord, ma'am."

She stood in silence, overwhelmed with Dudley's devotion to his friend. "You are a strange man, Dudley. Why would a man do so much for a friend?"

"For a man like Conner, that is simple and straight from the shoulder, there is nothing too good to be done for him. What I would do for him I believe he would willingly do for me. Be honest with me," said Dudley, "tell me if Conner means anymore to you than any stranger?"

"I hardly know him. How can I say?"

"You know him well enough to ask him to meet you in Dry Gulch the other day. You have seen him right here on this street. Come on now, you think something of him. What do you really think of him?"

"I think. I don't know."

"You know alright, does he seem like a genuine sort of fellow?"

"Yes, I suppose."

"The kind of man you could trust?"

"Yes, but…"

"Does he appear the kind who would stick to the girl he loved through thick and thin?"

THE GIRL WHO RODE INTO A STORM

"You mustn't talk like this," said Carmine as her voice trembled, but her eyes told him to go on.

"I'm going back and tell Conner, down in your heart, you have feelings for him. Maybe not as much as he has for you, but you have feelings that might grow one day into love."

"Don't say that. I, I, I am unsure."

"No you are not unsure, lady. I can see it in your eyes. When I tell him that you do have some feelings for him you can be assured that he is a man who will let loose with all he has to be with you, to take care of you, and, if there are barriers to being together he will leap those barriers no matter how high. He will not waver in his determination. That is the kind of man he is. That is why I admire him so."

She reached for his arm, clung to it in desperation. You tell him that and he will be murdered. He will come up against obstacles no man could climb over."

"You mean John Markham."

Bewildered, she said, "Yes, no, yes, no..."

"It is John Markham who is standing between you and Conner. I saw you in the street the other day, when you were talking to poor Conner. You looked back over your shoulder with incredible fear at that devil standing in the window of this house."

"Don't call him that!"

"I have talked to him, seen his manner, and I can say unequivocally that there is the devil in that man."

J. WAYNE FRYE   151

She was paralyzed with fear. "Are we quite alone?"

"Of course."

"Then he is a devil, and, being a devil, no ordinary man has a chance against him, not a chance. I don't know what you did in the house, but I think you must have outfoxed him in some way. You will pay for that I can assure you. And you'll pay with your life. Every minute now, you're in danger. You'll keep on being in danger, until he feels that he has squared his account with you. Don't you see that if I let Conner McCord come near me, the circumstance he'll face will be fatal for him?"

"O.K.," replied Dudley. "So, now the truth comes out. You do have feelings for Conner, which is why you are avoiding him."

"Ah, yes, I do! But, I cannot see him for that very reason."

"You have to see him, then. If you don't, he'll die trying to make it happen. He is a man with a strong will. I would rather see him dead than living the rest of his life, unhappy. He means that much to me."

She shook her head, arguing, and so they reached the end of the block without realizing it, then turned and strolled back toward the house. Still the girl argued, but it was in a whisper, as if she feared that John Markham might somehow be able to overhear them.

While all this was occurring, in the house Markham was still with Rena Tilson. They had gone to the lower floor den in the house, and sat silently by the fireplace. Markham looked over at her and said, "You're thinking of something."

"I'm sorry."

"You should be," he said.

He spoke without violence, as always, but she knew that he was intensely angry, and that familiar chill passed through her body. It never failed to come when she felt that she had aroused his anger.

"Why doesn't Carmine come back?" he asked

"She's letting him talk himself out. That's all. Carmine is clever. She knows how to let a man talk till his throat is dry, and then she'll smile and tell him that it's impossible to agree with him."

"I hope you are right," answered John Markham, and again there was that tightening of the muscles around his mouth. "He is like a gambler who has a certain way of masking his own face and looking at yours, as if he were dragging your thoughts out through your eyes; also, he's very cool; he belongs at a table with the cards on it where the stakes are high. There is something really strange about that man, something I just can't get my head around. His prissy manner makes him appear so benign, but under that effeminate exterior, in my opinion, beats the heart of a ferocious lion that would spring upon you in the blink of an eye. He is a man of contradictions, a man who makes me deeply suspicious of his real nature, of his real intentions. There just is something not right about him."

The door opened. "Here's Ralph. He'll tell us the truth of the matter. Has she come back?"

The young fellow kept far back in the shadow, and, when he spoke, his voice was uncertain, almost to the point of trembling. "No," he managed to say. "She ain't come back, chief."

Markham stared at him for a moment, waiting for more information. "Well," he said, and his words were violent and pointed, "come on you idiot, what did she do?"

"She went in the house across the street with that dandy-dressed man."

"He took her by force?" asked John Markham.

"Nope."

"Damn," shouted Markham. "Get out."

Markham stood up and paced quietly up and down the room. At length he turned abruptly to Rena. "Good night. I'm going out."

"What is it?" she asked eagerly.

He paused and angrily replied, "In the old days, when a man caught a poacher on his grounds, do you know what he did?"

"No."

"Shot him, or strung him up by a rope."

Rena was scared as she said, "You mean you are…"

"Shut up," he said as he walked out the door with anger in his heart.

Chapter 8
Fancy Peacock of a Man

Carmine stood in front of Conner's hotel room door trembling, as Dudley said, "Wait here while I go in and wake him up. It's going to be a big shock for him.

She stammered, "Are you sure he would even want to see me now after what happened outside the house the other day?"

"Life and love is a gamble. The world is like a reverse casino. In a casino, if you gamble long enough, you're certainly going to lose. In the real world, all you are gambling is your time or your embarrassment. Therefore, the more stuff you do, the more you give luck a chance to find you, the finer the rewards. Don't be afraid to lose when it comes to love; otherwise, you'll never find it."

"But I don't dare go in, not after what has happened."

Dudley put his hand softy on her shoulder as he said, "Too late to turn back now. Besides, in your heart of hearts, you don't want to turn back, you know that."

Quickly he passed into the room and hurried to Conner. He placed his right hand on his shoulder and shook him. Conner's eyes slowly opened and he said, "What's up?"

"Well, while you were sleeping I went across the street and brought somebody back."

"What?"

"Not what, but whom; Carmine Jones is waiting at the door. Go over and open it."

Suddenly wide awake, Conner, with deep emotion, said, "You've been the finest friend a man ever had, but, if this is a joke, you're in big trouble," and then he couldn't help himself. He just let it slip out without thinking. "I love you."

Dudley took a deep breath and looked at him with piecing, moist eyes. This was just something not said between two men in those days, even father and sons never said that, because it was considered unmanly. In a low, soft whisper, Dudley replied, "And I love you."

He then pointed toward the door and said, "Go let her in."

A somewhat shambled, dizzy Conner ambled to the door and opened it. As the light from the room struck down the hall, Dudley saw his friend stiffen to his full height and move a hand across his face.

THE GIRL WHO RODE INTO A STORM

Dudley turned his back to the two shocked people and went to the window. Across the street was the gloomy house of John Markham, and it seemed to be threatening Dudley like a clenched fist. The shadow under the upper gable was like the shadow under a frowning brow. In that house worked the mind of John Markham. Dudley knew there was trouble coming. He had won the first stage of the battle between them, but there was more to come, and who would win in the end was an open question. He made up his mind grimly that whatever happened he would first ship Conner and Carmine out of the city, then act as the rear guard to cover their retreat.

When he returned they had closed the door and were standing there in silence staring at one another. Conner glanced toward him and said, "You are a miracle man."

"There are no such things as miracles. There is just tenacity and hard work, and often they don't even pay off. I am happy I could do something for the both of you. Everyone deserves love without condition. In this world the church, the government, the society as a whole has to put qualifications on everything, even love. The church tells you to love only certain people that they decide are worthy. For example, two men or two women cannot, according to the church, love one another. Yet, the church is always talking about love, but doing very little to promote it. The government even charges for the privilege of getting a marriage licence, always barriers."

"I dunno how you did it," said an emotional Conner, "but here it is - done to perfection! You are amazing."

"A minute ago" said Dudley, "it looked like Carmine was unsure, but looking at the two of you now it is obvious her doubts have been curtailed."

"I found my own mind the moment I saw him," said Carmine.

"He has that effect on people," interjected Dudley, as he studied her in wonder. There was no hesitation on her part now as was evident in her demeanour. Suddenly, it seemed to Dudley that he had instantly become an old man, and these were two children under his protection. He struck into the heart of the problem at once with a pithy suggestion. "The main point," he said, "is to get you two out of town, as quickly as we can. In Montana he can take care of you, but here John Markham is a devil and has the strength to stop both of you. How quickly can you go, Carmine?"

"I can never go," she said, "as long as John Markham is alive."

"Then he's as good as dead," said Conner. "We both got guns, and we know how to use them if anybody tries to prevent you from leaving."

Carmine shook her head. All the joy had gone out of her face and left her wistful and misty eyed. "You don't understand, and I can't tell you. You can never harm John Markham."

"Why not," demanded Conner as his neck veins bulged from building anger.

"He is a man I cannot escape."

"Why not?" asked Conner. "Has he got a hundred men around him all the time? Even if he has there's ways of getting at him."

"He doesn't need help. He never fails. He is known as the man who never loses."

"Listen to me," said Dudley angrily. "Seems to me that everybody stands around in fear of this man without what I can see any real reasons to do so. As for never losing, look where you are now. Tonight he lost you."

"No, he hasn't lost me. I have to go back."

"Why?" demanded Conner.

Analyzing the situation, Dudley said, "It's because of you, Conner. If she leaves, Markham will come after you, and that will put you in harm's way."

"I'm not afraid of him," shouted Conner.

"I know that," said a troubled Dudley, "and I am mulling over just how we can best this man. It won't be easy. This is a hard man."

"Don't you see?" asked Carmine. "Both of you are strong men and brave, but against John Markham I know that you're helpless. It isn't the first time people have hated him. Who does anything but hate him? But that doesn't make any difference. He wins, he always wins, and that's why I've come to you. I want to save you from harm." She then turned to Conner, with a sad resignation in her eyes as she continued "I've come to tell you that I can love you, that I knew that right away when we corresponded. All of your kindness showed through your letters, plain and strong and simple and true. I've come tonight to tell you that I can love you, but that I dare not for fear of what might happen. Not that I fear him for myself, but for you."

"Listen," said Conner. "Ain't there police in this town?"

"What could they do? In all of the things which he has done no one has been able to accuse him of a single illegal act, at least no one has ever been able to prove a thing. And yet he lives by crime. Does that give you an idea of the sort of man he is?"

"Yes," replied Conner, "the kind of man who probably has the authorities in his pocket; the kind who appeals to people's greed. The police don't protect the poor. They protect the wealthy."

"Tell us straight up Carmine," said Dudley, "what sort of a hold does he have over you?"

"I will tell you," said Carmine with deep emotion, "if you insist, but won't you take my word for it and ask no more?"

"We have a right to know," replied Dudley. "We are ready to stand up to him for you. We should know for that reason alone. He is using you, Carmine. We know that, but we need an explanation, because without that we are entering the fray like blind men.

She nodded in resignation that she owed them the truth. "If I tell you that, you both will hate me. You will both think me horrible."

"Try us," said Dudley. "The greatest moral failing is to condemn someone or something without understanding the circumstances. I am sure I speak for Conner too when I say that."

Conner, nodding his head in agreement, added, "What you do may be bad; but I saw from your contriteness in that second letter the kind of person you really are. The inside of you is right, Carmine, no matter what John Markham makes you do. I, like Dudley, am not one to judge someone unless that person is judgmental, and then I have a problem. I have watched finger-pointers all my life, and the truth be known, I ain't got no use for them at all. Until you have walked in another man's or woman's shoes, you best keep your judgmental attitudes to yourself."

Dudley looked at Conner with admiration, because that was why he cared so much for him. This was a man with a heart. He added, "Go ahead and tell us Carmine, we are here to help not judge."

Tears swelled up in her eyes as she said, "He has made me a prostitute and a thief. There you have it, the truth."

Dudley saw Conner wince, as if someone had struck him a hard blow. And he himself waited, curious to see what the big fellow would do. He had not long to wait. Conner went straight to the girl and took her hands, holding them delicately and kindly. Then he wrapped her in his arms as she cried, and said, "It's O.K. Don't worry. You are with friends now, and we are here to help you, not judge you. Don't think that makes any difference to us? Not to me, and not to my friend

Dudley. There's something behind it. Tell us what it is."

"Yes, there is something behind it," said contrite sounding Carmine. "I can't say how grateful I am to you both for still trusting me. I have a brother. He came to Denver to work, and found it was easy to spend money. He spent it very foolishly. Finally he began sending home for money. My family is not rich, but we gave him what we could. It went on like that for some time. Then, one day, a stranger called at our house, and it was John Markham. He wanted to see me, and, when we talked together, he told me that my brother had done a terrible thing, but I will not tell you what it was. I wouldn't believe him at first, though he showed me what looked like proof. At last I believed enough to agree to go to Denver and see for myself. I came here, and saw my brother and made him confess. As I said, I will not reveal what it was. I can only say that his life is in the hands of John Markham because of what he has done. John Markham has only to say a few words, and my brother is dead. He told me that. He showed me the hold that Markham had over him, and begged me to do what I could for him. I didn't see how I could be of use to him, but Markham showed me how I could help. He taught me to steal, and I have stolen. He taught me to lie, and I have lied. He taught me to let men use me for pleasure. Men he picked and was paid by. And he has me in the palms of his hands? And that's why I say that it's hopeless. Even if you could fight against him, which no one can, you couldn't help me. The moment you strike him he strikes my brother."

"Don't be so sure all is lost, Carmine," said an angered Dudley. "There is one thing to do. First of all you have to go back to John Markham. Tell him that you came over here. Tell him that you saw Conner, but you only came to say good-bye to him, and to ask him to leave town and to leave you alone. Then, tomorrow, we'll move out, and hopefully he may think that we've gone. Meantime, the thing you do is to give me the name of your brother and tell me where I can find him. I'll hunt him up. Maybe something can be done for him. I don't know, but that's where we've got to start."

"But, but…"

Conner interrupted her and said, "Listen to him. I tell you that this is a person who stands by his word. Do what he says. I've doubted him before, but look at all that he's done out of friendship for me. Do what he says, Carmine."

"I trust you. I will do as you say. Give me a slip of paper, and I'll write on it what you need to know about my brother's location."

Into the night from that house went Carmine with growing determination. She glanced warily about her. The street was empty, quieter than when she had left. She knew perfectly well that John Markham had not allowed her to be gone so long without keeping watch over her. Somewhere on that street Markham's spies kept guard over her movements. She glanced sharply over her shoulder, and it seemed to her that a shadow flitted into the door of a basement farther up the street.

At that, she scurried across the street. She paused with her hand upon the knob. To enter meant to step back into the life which she hated. There had been a time when she had almost loved the life to which John Markham introduced her; there had been a time when she had rejoiced in the nimbleness of her body which had enabled her to become adept at thievery and prostitution. And, by so doing, she had kept the life of her brother from danger, she believed. She was still helping him, and, so long as she worked for John Markham, she knew that her brother was safe. Yet she hesitated at the door, because worse than being a thief was the degradation she felt when she was forced to satisfy the lust of men Markham brought to her. She hesitated, but knew that she might be on the path to being saved from this wretched existence. Still, the thought of how she must endure the misery inside that house kept her from turning the knob. It would be only the work of a moment to flee back to the men across the street that offered her hope, tell them that she could not and dared not stay longer with the reprehensible John Markham. Her hand fell from the knob, but she raised it again immediately when she realized that Markham had the power of life or death over her brother. If the two men, as promised, were able to inspire her brother with the courage to flee from Denver, give up his high life and seek refuge in some far-off place, then she would go with Conner to the ends of the earth and mock the cunning fiend who had controlled her life for so long.

The important thing now was to disarm him of all suspicion, make him feel that she had only visited Conner in order to say farewell to him. With this in her mind, she opened the front door and stepped into the foyer, which was always lighted with ominous dimness. That gloom fell about her like the visible presence of John Markham who stood like a mighty sphinx staring across the desert sand.

When we imagine something wicked and full of vice, we tend to use inaccurate visual shorthand. All too often we think of evil as something ugly, dark and scary. We see it as something that leaves a mark on the flesh that can be detected by mere looks. We actually expect images of evil to look malevolent and abnormal, as a comforting sign that the evil ones are physically totally different from the rest of us, allowing us to believe that humanity as a whole is not wretched and irredeemable. Yet, the banker with immaculately coiffured hair and toned features sitting behind a desk in his fine suit can destroy more people with a pen than a wild-eye terrorist can with a machine-gun. A cleric with a sharp tongue of condemnation can shred decency with lips that spew more evil than the devil could muster from the fiery pits of hell. Evil actually has no face. It is the person next door, the individual whom you have known all your life, the policeman, the teacher, the gardener, any number of people who just appear normal but within harbour an uncontrollable urge to embrace the dark side.

Markham was a bulk of man. He stood 6:2 and was stern looking with a certain Savoir-faire about him. He was a powerful looking figure with an air of arrogance. He stared at Carmine with piercing eyes as he said, "Welcome back, bitch."

In the past, the violence of his language had given her clues enough to the workings of his mind. She had always been a favoured member of the gang, and the men whom she had dallied with found her ravishing and it had put Markham in good stead with them for providing such a fine woman for their pleasure. A sudden weakness came over her, as Markham said, "We've all taken lip enough from you. Your day's over."

She moved slowly to the stairs. With her hand on the balustrade she decided to try the effect of one personal appeal. "I'm terribly afraid!" she said with great trepidation,

"Are you?" asked Markham. "Well, you better be," he said in a cold, soft, monotone voice, as he pointed toward the den to her right, indicating she should go in, which she did, followed by him.

She stood trembling as he sat down in a deep easy-chair. His dressing gown and horn-rimmed spectacles gave him a look of owlish wisdom. He rose from the chair. She thought at first, as he pointed to another chair, that he was going to take his usual damnable tack of pretended ignorance in order to see how much she would confess. However, tonight this was not his plan of attack.

THE GIRL WHO RODE INTO A STORM

The moment she was seated, he removed his spectacles and placed them on an end table, drew up a cane-backed chair close to hers and sat down, leaning far forward. "Now my dear foolish girl," he said smiling benevolently at her, "what have you been doing tonight to make me regret letting you leave with that cretin?"

She knew at once that he was aware of every move she had made, from the first to the last, but she was preparing a master lie. "It's a very unusual yarn, John," she said.

"I'm used to crazy tales," he answered. "But where have you been all this time? It was only to take five minutes, I thought."

She made herself laugh. "That's because you don't know Dudley Danforth."

"I'm getting to know him," said Markham. "And, before I'm through, I will know him a lot better, and he will know me, and he will regret the day he entered this house."

"Well, he is a persuasive guy."

"I'll grant him that."

"And, when he told me how poor Conner McCord had come all the way from Dry Gulch to see me. Well, I was touched because Dudley made it such a sad affair that I promised I'd go across the street and see Conner."

"In his room?"

"Where else? I knew you wouldn't let him come to see me here."

"Never presuppose on my actions my dear little girl."

She eyed him shrewdly, but, if there was any deception in him, he hid it well. "I went there, however," she said, "because I was sorry for him, John. If you had seen you'd have been sorry, too, or else you would have laughed; I could hardly keep from it at first."

"I suppose he took you in his arms?"

"I think he wanted to. Then, of course, I told him at once why I had come."

"Which was?"

"Simply that it was absurd for him to pursue me and that the letters I wrote him were simply written for fun during my vacation, when I was doing some of my cousin's work at the correspondence school; and that the best thing he could do would be to take my apology and go back home, but he was full of pride, and gave me a lecture about deceiving men."

"So, you have no interest in him?"

"Well, I have a mild interest. That's all, though."

Coldly, Markham interjected a note of fear. "I was worried so much about you and this foolish fellow that I gave orders for him to be put out of the way, as soon as you left him."

She quickly stood for a moment stunned and looked down at him pleading, "No, no, no! I'm sorry."

"Sorry doesn't cut it around here."

"Please call him back, the one you sent. Call him back, John, and I'll serve you the rest of my life without question. I'll never fail you, John, but please don't have him killed."

THE GIRL WHO RODE INTO A STORM

"I thought it would be this way," he said coldly. "You told a very good lie. I suppose Dudley Danforth rehearsed you in it, but I can read your lies like a book. I sent nobody. I just wanted to see the truth. You have feelings for this Conner guy, and if you follow through on them, he'll pay the price. Do you want that?"

"No, no, please. I am sorry."

"Get to your room," he said fiercely. "I've wasted too much time on you and your brother. I've a mind to wash my hands of all of you. Get to your room, and stay there, while I make up my mind just what I am going to do."

She went, cringing with fear as he shouted after her, "Brother or lover, which shall it be?"

She turned and stretched out her hands to him, unable to speak; but he laughed in her face. In mute terror, she slumped her shoulders and went wearily away.

Back across the street, Conner was pacing up and down as he said, "I have forgotten Deanna now. I am over her. This is the girl for me."

Sullen, with a frown on his lips, Dudley said, "Oh, you are that fickle. You now turn your back on a woman you adored a short while ago."

"What are you saying? You brought the girl here. You assailed Deanna as not attainable. Now are you telling me I am too fickle when you encouraged me to move on from my fascination with Deanna?"

"You are right Conner. I did encourage you to forget her, but I wonder if she can forget you."

"Why would you say that? Do you know something about her that I don't?"

"I know that she obviously is enamoured with you, but apparently thinks a relationship is beyond the realm of possibility. I stand corrected. You should forget her. Yes."

Dudley stood and contemplated. His morose look bothered Conner and he asked, "There is something you aren't telling me. Please don't keep me in the dark."

"Fate is a cruel master my friend. I am getting bad feelings. There are signs I sense of impending doom."

"What? What are you fearful of?"

"I am fearful of what might happen to you. I am fearful of Deanna who keeps popping in and out of your life. Most of all, I am fearful of the man across the street who embodies the dark side of humanity. He is not one with whom you should idly trifle. That is a man capable of unspeakable evil. It is bedtime; we'll talk in the morning."

Dudley said goodnight, walked to the window, stood with his hand on the sill, looked back at Conner and said "I have a lot of scars, Conner. More than you will ever know. I carry a secret that tears at my insides, but I can reveal it to no one. I want you happy, and if this girl can make you happy I will do all I can to help the two of you. In a way, helping you two find conjugal bliss is the same as me finding it."

"You'll find it too, Dudley. I know you will, a fine fellow like you."

"No Conner, I will never marry. I have known that almost my entire life. That is for others, not me."

Conner sensed a defeatist attitude on the part of Dudley, an attitude he had seen no evidence of before. "It'll be alright Dudley. We gonna see this thing through and then all will be O.K."

"Maybe not and maybe so, I am not a prophet, but I don't like what I see in that man Markham's eyes. I think he is holding back some cards on us, and I would sure like to see the cards he is holding. What I'm going to work for is this, Conner: To get Carmine's brother, Jerry Jones, and rustle him out of town. I think if he is clear of this place, Markham will fold."

"But how can you do that when Markham has a hold on him?"

"I think Markham is bluffing. He can't turn anyone over to the police, because it would implicate him. He has been fronting Carmine's brother money. I see her brother as a self-serving, selfish miscreant. He may have even put Markham up to using him to get his sister to do their bidding. He may be splitting the profits with Markham from her prostituting herself. Anyway, we'll get hold of him and wake him up and pay off his debts to Markham, which most likely run to several thousand dollars if he is on the level and is really in hock to him."

"How?"

"Hey, you've seen Deanna gamble. Well, I am as good as she is. Easy money for me."

THE GIRL WHO RODE INTO A STORM

"Once we get Jerry Jones, then the whole gang of us will head straight for Montana, as fast as we can. Goodnight."

Watching Dudley pace up and down proclaiming he was as good a gambler as Deanna made Conner reflect on a woman who just a few days before had walked in and out of his life in a fashion that bordered on the fanciful. He wondered what secret about Deanna Dudley was harbouring. He could have asked, but why should he? He had given up on Deanna and put all his hopes on the nearly equally mysterious Carmine. He thought to himself that the only real thing he could count on in life was his dear new friend, Dudley. He considered the friendship between them so profound they had almost become one soul dwelling in two bodies.

Never had the mind of Dudley worked more quickly and surely as when he met Jerry Jones. The case of Jones was exactly as he surmised. As for the crime of which John Markham knew, and held like a club over Jerry, it had been purely and simply an act of self-defence. But, to Carmine and her brother, Markham had made it seem clear the shadow of the hangman's rope was before him.

Markham had worked seriously to win control of Carmine. She was remarkably dexterous; she was the soul of courage; and, he was making a fortune off a beautiful woman. In the meantime, she did well for herself, too, and he strengthened his hold on her through her brother. It was not hard to do. If Jerry was the soul of recklessness, he also was

J. WAYNE FRYE

the soul of misery in many ways. John Markham had only to lead the boy toward a life of heavy expenditures and gambling, lending him, from time to time, the money to keep it up. It was easy to control the life of such a vulnerable person. However, now, Dudley had entered into the picture and everything was about to change. Still, Markham was one step ahead so he thought, because he had plans to send Jerry out of town on an errand for him. He would not risk the effect of Dudley's smooth tongue.

Very early the next morning John Markham went straight to Jerry's apartment. It was his own man, Norman Krupp, who answered the bell and opened the door to him. He had supplied Krupp as a butler to Jerry, immediately after he had Carmine occupy a man in a dalliance while a confederate stole some jewels from a safe in the home. That clever piece of work had proved the worth of the girl and made it necessary to spare no expense on Jerry. So he had given him the tried and proven Norman.

The moment he looked into the grinning face of Norman he knew that the master was not at home, and both the chief and the servant relaxed. They were friends of too long a term to stand on ceremony.

"There's no one here?" asked Markham.

"He's gone, skipped out."

Markham was puzzled. "When is he coming back?"

"Didn't leave any word, chief."

THE GIRL WHO RODE INTO A STORM

"Isn't this earlier than his usual time for starting the day?"

"Usually not out of bed before noon."

"What happened this morning?"

"Something rare, something it would have done your heart good to see!"

"Go on."

"I was rousted out of bed at eight by the intercom. The desk clerk downstairs said a gentleman was calling on Mr. Jones. I said, of course, that Mr. Jones couldn't be called on at that hour. Then the clerk said the gentleman would come up to the door and explain. I told him to come ahead. Was a prissy kind of fellow come to the door. Didn't give a name. 'I've come to surprise Jerry, he says to me.' I told him it was too early for a surprise. Then he said this was going to be one of the exceptions. He kept insisting. Smooth talker he was. So I say O.K., but mind yourself, cause he is liable to wake up swinging this early."

A concerned look on his face, Markham said, "And he went in?"

"What's wrong with that?" asked Norman anxiously.

"Go ahead."

"Well, in he went to Jerry's room. I listened at the door. I heard him call Jerry, and then Jerry groaned like he was half dead. Jerry says, 'I don't know you. Get the devil outta my room before I mop the floor up with you. You disturbing a man who needs his sleep.' Then all hell broke lose."

THE GIRL WHO RODE INTO A STORM

"I heard the springs squeak, as Jerry jumped out of bed. I heard a thud, and I opened the door. What I see was Jerry lying flat, and this guy sitting on his chest, as calm and smiling as you please. I closed the door quickly. Jerry's too game a boy to mind being licked fair and square, but, of course, he'd rather fight until he died than have me or anybody else see him give up, so I thought it best not to enter."

Norman took a deep breath and continued. "Jerry tells him to wait and he'll get dressed. Guess he developed some respect for the guy since he bested him, which few have physically done. I sensed the two of them are developing mutual respect, so I went away from the door and didn't listen any more, and in about half an hour out they walk, arm in arm, like old pals."

It was perfectly clear to John Markham that Dudley had come there purposely to break the link between him and young Jerry Jones.

"How much does Jerry owe me?" he asked of Norman suddenly.

Norman took out a pad and calculated for a moment: "Four thousand eight hundred and forty-two."

Upset that he had gotten there too late, Markham said, "Listen, if he comes back, which I doubt, keep him here. Get him away from this guy Dudley no matter what you have to do. In any case, if he comes back here, don't let him get away. You understand?"

"Nope, but I don't need to understand. I'll do it."

THE GIRL WHO RODE INTO A STORM

Markham did not like being bested by anyone. And, being beaten by a frilly-dressed gay blade of a man was particularly displeasing to him.

He strolled out into the street, looked at the people scurrying about, all of whom he saw as sheep ripe for fleecing. They followed a creed that had brainwashed them into believing they lived in a country where opportunity was unlimited. Well, it was for people like Markham, who knew the truth. America was a nation of robber barons who bought politicians like any other commodity. He had bought plenty himself. He sighed deeply and headed back home determined to turn the situation around. Yep, he was not going to be bested by an effeminate-looking fancy peacock of a man.

J. WAYNE FRYE

Chapter 9
Stare with Shock at Her

Only the select few could afford to gamble at Fernando's. He was rarely crooked; and yet he would not have a dealer in his employ unless the fellow knew every good trick of manipulating the deck. The reason was that, while Fernando preferred not to cheat in order to take money away from his customers, he very frequently had his men cheat in order to give money away. This sounds like a mad procedure for the proprietor of a gaming house, but there were profound reasons beneath it. For one of the maxims of Fernando, whose real name was Fred, was that the best way to make a man lose money is first of all to make him win it. It is what was called in the 1980's by the man referred to as a marketing genius by the

THE GIRL WHO RODE INTO A STORM

Los Angeles Times, Wayne Frye, as the carrot carousel of calamitous copulation of the mind. You make a man think he is in control by dangling the idea he is a winner in front of him and before he knows it he has allowed himself to be manipulated into a maniacal obsession that the more he spends the more he wins. This is the apex of a society where everyone is taught that you are judged by the size of your bank account not the size of your character. In the America of the 1890's this was true, and it is still true today as Americans are the easiest people to manipulate in the world through a variety of means that plays upon their propensity for believing in their own infallibility and superiority, when in fact the truth is that there is absolutely nothing superior in the way they are so easily propagandized and manipulated.

Thus was it made easy for Frederic Fernando Ferro to effectively pick the pockets of people in such a way that they actually seemed happy to hand over their money. He was a man who knew how to effectively bleed his customers to economic death. To help, he had selected two men, both young, both shrewd, both iron in will and nerve and courage, both apparently equally expert with the cards, and both just as equally capable of utilizing the skills needed to drain customer funds slowly and effectively. One was Timothy McIver, the other was Terry Smothers.

On this night, McIver was dealing at one of the tables, and Smothers stood at the side of Fernando.

THE GIRL WHO RODE INTO A STORM

Now and again Smother's dark eyes wandered toward the table where McIver sat, with the cards flashing through his fingers. McIver loved the feel of the polished cardboard under his finger tips that made him a king. To him, poker was not just a card game. It was a way of life.

As he watched, Smothers noticed the smooth skill with which McIver buried a card. Yet, the trick was not perfectly done. Had he, Smothers, been there he would have done it much more efficiently.

Fernando said to Smothers, "This is a nuisance," as he watched a familiar face stroll into the establishment. With him, the man with the familiar face had a fancy dressed dude who looked like a peacock in full-bloom. He knew Jerry Jones, but was not familiar with his companion.

"Another table and dealer wasted," declared Fernando. "Jones and he's brought some friend of his with him!"

"Shall I see if I can turn them away without playing?" asked Smothers.

"No, not yet. Jones is a friend of John Markham's. Don't forget that. Never forget that friends of John Markham have to be handled gently."

"I understand."

"I'll see how far I can go with them," Fernando said as he got up and went behind the bar where he picked up the relatively new invention that a few of the more affluent had embraced with glee. On the Bell-a-Phone as the telephone was called at the time, he rang another member of the Denver fringe-class elite, John Markham.

"How far should I go with them?" he asked, after he had explained that Jones had just come in.

"And who is with him?" asked John Markham eagerly.

"A fancy dude in frilly dress about his age," said Fernando.

"That's the man I want!"

"The man you want?"

"No time to explain, but my guess is that the fancy dressed one is probably good at cards."

"Look," replied Fernando, "I have been your proxy bank for a long time, but this Jones character is a little bit tiresome."

"Stop complaining, you have made a lot of money off me."

"Of course, how much shall I allow them to win?"

"Win, no, bleed them both dry. Let them play on credit. Go as far as you like, but nail them good."

"I'll put my best man on it then."

Markham added, "I'll be by in awhile."

The face of Fernando was dark when he went back to Smothers. "What do you think of the fellow with Jerry Jones?" he asked.

"Of him?" asked Smothers with a smirk on his face. "That is about the fanciest dressed dude I ever seen. That ain't a man, that's a peacock prancing about displaying his fine feathers like he is looking for a mate, only this dude here is looking for a mate of the same sex, maybe Jones."

THE GIRL WHO RODE INTO A STORM

Dudley was idling at a table close to the wall, running his hands through a litter of cards and dice piled on a table. He raised his head suddenly and glanced across the room at Smothers with his piercing, dark brown eyes and flipped his hands though his long, lustrous dark hair that was in a ponytail as it glistened against the white wall behind him while his eyes lingered on Smothers and seemed to pass a harsh judgement on him. Smothers could actually feel the chill of contempt.

Smothers was not intimidated at all but was curious. There was something about this fellow, or his opinion would not have been asked. What was it?

"Well?" asked Fernando peevishly. "So, you think this guy is a bit of a dandy, then?"

"I think," said Smothers rather casually, "that he'd look better in a fancy, frilly dress than what he's wearing, but I also sense very profoundly that he is not a man to be trifled with. Just like a woman in frills, buckles and bows can be deadlier than a man with a gun; this fancy dude is probably a fair hand with that gun he has strapped to his hip. It is best I would think, despite his looks, to be leery of him."

"Well, I've an idea that you think right. There's something about him that says be cautious. The way he looks about, so slowly that is the way a fearless man is apt to look. Do you think you can sit at the table with the man called Dudley Danforth by Markham and Jerry Jones and win from them this evening?"

"Don't I always win when told to? I only lose on orders from you."

"Tonight Smothers it's going to be your work to make all the luck come to you. Do you think you can?"

A faint smile began to dawn on Smothers' face. Never in his life had he heard news so sweet to his ears. It meant, in brief, that he was to be trusted for the first time at real manipulation of the cards. His trust in himself was complete. This would be a crushing blow for Dudley and Jones.

"Mind yourself," said Fernando, "if you are caught at cheating, you'll cause me a lot of trouble."

Just then, Dudley went over and whispered something to Jerry Jones, and he made his way toward the door while Jerry continued playing poker. Dudley looked back at Smothers and waved goodbye as he pranced out of the casino.

"What the...," shouted Fernando. "We just lost our pigeon."

Fernando jumped up, went behind the bar for the phone and called Markham. There was shock from him, but he told Fernando to watch carefully and tell him what was happening with Jones.

Fernando held the phone and described to Markham every move being made by Jones. This went on for about five minutes until Conner McCord strolled in and walked over to speak to Jones. He sat down and started playing. Fernando described McCord to Markham, who instantly told Fernando to break them both.

THE GIRL WHO RODE INTO A STORM

There is an interval when something magical happens on the plains of time. There is that one moment when all the stars are perfectly lined up to shine the bright light of destiny down from the heavens and everyone in a certain place knows they are about to witness something grand and glorious. It was as if time suddenly stood still, as no one moved, even the dealers stopping to look in astonishment, because there she was. Strolling through the swinging doors was the most incredibly beautiful woman to ever grace the casino. A vision of lace and flesh with clicking heels glided across the room as light collected around her body like it was finding a warm place to call home. She moved not like a mortal, but as though she bore an angel's form and her wings were flapping a melody of sensual delight. Her light blue dress was tied boldly about her thin waist and her bosom was as a bird's chest, soft and slight, but of such an appealing form that one could not help but let eyes linger upon those rising and falling orbs wondering how spongy, delicate and velvety they must be to the touch.

Everyone there looked and looked, knowing clearly that on this day a memory would be branded into their brains of this one moment in their lives. She was everything a man could hope for in a woman. She was the faint violet whiff of the morning dew. She was the rising sun that would warm the day. She was the echo on the brink of a dangerous ravine. She was a blazing fire with flames soaring skyward. She was the gilded cage where a bird would give up flight to be imprisoned for a moment basking in her glorious light that shined from her dark brown eyes and twinkled like a million stars.

Her hair was the colour of raven's wings and cascaded like a waterfall half way down her back. She overflowed with apparent peace, wisdom and compassion. She did not appear to walk as she moved toward the poker table where a mesmerized Conner sat staring, she glided. She looked directly at Conner and smiled as her eyes danced with a dreamy look that said, "I'm here and I am yours." Yes, Deanna Defoe was back!

She walked up to Conner and tapped him on the shoulder. She said softly and seductively, "Get up and give me your seat. Dudley sent me to do what he was going to do. He is on another mission right now."

"You have finally met Dudley?"

"I have, and he knows I am better than he is. So good that I can accomplish the task you two set out to accomplish here with Jerry Jones," she said as Conner got up.

Deanna leaned over and whispered something to Jerry, who smiled and nodded his head in an affirmative manner. While all this was going on, Fernando was describing the scene to Markham, who bellowed out, "I know that woman. She has worked the gambling halls all over Montana and Colorado with skill. She is hard to beat. Do you have a man who can do it?"

"Same guy who was going to play Danforth."

THE GIRL WHO RODE INTO A STORM

"Get the job done," demanded Markham. "She is in cahoots with them. They are playing a dangerous game with me."

Fernando nodded to Smothers, who got up and walked over to McIver's table, placing his hand on his shoulder. McIver got up, and as Smothers sat down, he looked directly at Deanna and said, "Gentleman, and lady, of course, I'll be your new dealer, and what about a higher table limit so we can make the game a little more interesting.

All agreed to actually take off the limit, and make it a no-holds barred game. Conner pulled up a chair from a nearby table and sat behind Deanna. He was curious as to how Dudley had managed to meet her, and to enlist her in their cause. Now, again, he faced a dilemma. He looked at Deanna and knew that if it came down to a meaningful choice, he would pick Deanna over Carmine, but it had been made clear to him by Deanna that she was but a passing fancy who offered him no credible future. Still, he was fascinated by her, and felt the same friendship had been forged between them that had developed between he and Dudley. O.K., maybe it was a bit more intimate a friendship than that which he shared with Dudley, and at that thought, he could not resist reaching over and lightly touching Deanna on the shoulder. She turned and looked at him. He could not help but quiver. To look into those eyes was to teeter on the brink of an abyss. When she fixed that gaze upon anyone, they knew instantly they were in danger of falling. They resisted as there was a danger about her that was unmistakeable, but they all succumbed to her charms. Her magnetism was irresistible, and all were weapon-less in the face of it. This was a woman who was like an opened box of TNT, and she had a match in her hand that she might strike at any second.

The struggle of all fundamentally honest people to make a decent living in a corrupt, uncaring society like America's is an almost impossible task, and the only winners are usually those at the top of the economic ladder, but occasionally there are a few who penetrate through the veil that protects the privileged, and Fernando had penetrated that veil, but had done it with Markham's help, so even though he was now part of the economic elite, he still had to pay his dues to Markham. That is why Smothers was at that table trying to rein in those who were opposing Markham. He and his boss were beholding to a miscreant of mayhem who had them enslaved to serve his interests first and foremost. This was the way of a world that crushed those in the middle and the bottom in order to provide a life of luxury for those at the top.

The game opened slowly. The first, second, and third hands were won by Jerry Jones. He tucked away his chips with a smile of satisfaction, as if the three hands were significant of the whole progress of the game. But Deanna Defoe accepted her losses with neither smile nor sneer. She had played too often in games which she realized were based on the ebb and flow of fortune. Miners had come in with their belts loaded with gold dust, eager to bet the entire sum of their winnings on one spin of the roulette wheel. Ranchers, fat with the profits of a good sale of cattle, had wagered the whole amount of the take in the hopes of turning a meagre profit into a fortune. This was the way of those who believed lady luck might smile on them, but the truth was lady luck was nothing but a fickle mistress. Meanwhile, as all those at the table kept cutting an eye to observe the beautiful Deanna, who was sustaining some modest losses, she was observing the skill of Smothers.

She surmised that he was playing the game too conservatively. Stacking the deck of cards with the adeptness which years of practice had given to him, he never raised the amount of his opponent's hand beyond its own order. A pair was beaten by a pair, three of a kind was simply beaten by three of a kind of a higher order; and, when a full house was permitted by his expert dealing to appear to excite the other gamblers, he himself indulged in no more than a superior grade of three of a kind. Half a dozen times coincidences happened without calling for any distrust on the part of the players, but eventually Deanna postulated where this was leading. Training enabled her eyes to do what the eyes of the ordinary person could not achieve, and, while to Jerry Jones all that happened in the deals of Smothers was the height of correctness, Deanna, at the seventh deal, awakened to the fact that something was very wrong.

THE GIRL WHO RODE INTO A STORM

She waited and watched, hoping that Jerry Jones might also pick up on the fraud which was being perpetrated on them. But Jones maintained a bland interest in the game. He had won between two and three thousand dollars at this point and these winnings had been allowed by the very skilled Smothers to accumulate in little runs, here and there. For nothing encourages a gambler toward reckless betting so much as a few series of high hands. He then begins to believe that he can tell, by some mysterious feeling inside, that one good hand presages another. Jerry Jones had not been brought to the point where he was willing to plunge, but he was getting very close to it.

Smothers was gathering the youngster into a web of deceit, and Deanna, fully awake and aware of all that was happening, felt a gathering rage accumulating in her. The winnings of Jones were carefully balanced against the losses of Deanna Defoe. She was gradually preparing for war, but like a scout sent to reconnoitre before a great battle, she was slowly plotting her strategy.

It was at this point that Rena Tilson, with a smooth rustling of her silk evening dress like the stir of gentle breeze walked into the establishment. She was not as captivating as Deanna, but she did catch the attention of the men there to the point that Deanna noticed Smothers was using her attention grabbing, which was distracting the players, to actually deal from the bottom of the deck. There was a seething rage building within her.

THE GIRL WHO RODE INTO A STORM

It was almost immediately evident to Deanna that this was what Rena did in service to John Markham and Fernando. Her chosen work under their direction was to distract players so they could be more easily fleeced. The uneasy fire was in her eyes, the same fire that she had seen used time and again. She moved behind the players at the table, glancing at their cards and the blinking of her eyes was a signal to Smothers of what hands the players held.

She, with what appeared to be a tinge of jealousy in her demeanour, looked at Deanna with discordant derision. Deanna did not hide her cards from view, as she was laying her trap.

There was a vacant chair at the table, and in order to dull the edge caused by her observational cheating, Deanna pointed at the open chair and said, "Have a seat and join us in a grand game of chance," then she looked directly at Smothers with piercing eyes just to let him know she knew what was going on. She continued "because we have a fine dealer, who has mastered the fine art of dealing so well that it is like watching Renoir paint one of his masterpieces."

"No thanks," she said, then with her eyes indicated Deanna should follow her to the bar.

Deanna excused herself and went over to the bar. She leaned next Rena and whispered, "You have something to share with me?"

"I have bad news," she whispered instantly, "but keep smiling. This place is full of Markham's spies. About an hour ago I ran into Dudley

THE GIRL WHO RODE INTO A STORM

Danforth outside when I was on my way to the ice cream shop across the street. He told me that there would eventually be a beautiful lady playing cards in here, and that I should make sure not to let them snooker you, because he knew I was a shill for the gamblers in here. John Markham is out for you now probably, because you are helping Jerry Jones. Why, in heaven's name, are you interfering? It will be your death. I promise you. John Markham has placed men around the casino. He means business. Help yourself if you can. I'm unable to lift a hand for you. If I were you I should leave, and I should leave at once. This will not end well for you, Conner McCord, Jerry Jones or your friend Dudley. He is a fine person. A bit on the unusual side, but I find him attractive and appealing."

"I'll leave now. Good luck," said Rena.

She watched her going, but was not driven to fear by what she said. She went back to her place at the table, still smiling in apparent enjoyment of what she had just heard. She saw Smother's glance of interrogation and distrust, a typical thief's suspicion of an honest person. She was dealt the cards and she swept up her hand, bet a hundred, with apparently foolish recklessness, on three sevens, and then had to buy fresh chips from Smothers. She was moving in for the kill now.

Fernando, glancing in the direction of the game from time to time, watched the demolition of Deanna's pile of chips, with growing joy, because he knew she was allied with Jones.

J. WAYNE FRYE

THE GIRL WHO RODE INTO A STORM

Conner stared in amazement at the cool demeanour of Deanna as she seemed un-phased by her losses. He saw her as a tower of strength who would not bend before adversity. The end of a bad situation can often be sensed in the mind of the astute observer as a glint of light at the end of a dark tunnel. Whether the end is positive or negative though can rarely be ascertained as someone once said that light at the end of the proverbial tunnel might be a fright train of misery headed your way. Deanna had agreed to help thought Conner as Dudley had finally met her by chance and realized obviously that she was a superior card player to him and offered a better chance at success.

Despite his penchant to always do as Markham requested, Fernando could not help but admire the lady who was obviously there to do him in. She was not only beautiful, but had a deadly countenance about her. This was a woman who was a cool as iced tea on a hot summer day.

When she kept losing, it was obvious that despite her coolness, she was running out of options. She raised from her seat slowly her lips parting as if puckering for a deep, passionate kiss and pulled up the left side of her dress to her thighs. A hush fell over the place as the sight of that magnificent leg penetrated the 400 eyes in the room and nearly blinded the observers with its brightness. It was more than just a leg. Its smoothness, its symmetrical perfection was like observing a fine sculpture in a museum.

Conner had ravelled in ecstasy the few times he had been blessed and allowed to fondle and caress that body in a few well-defined places, but right there in that moment he shivered with amazement as her powerful, taunt, muscular leg that contracted in delight at the same time as his own heart contracted with desire. The athletic, muscular leg decorated her body as a gorgeous pearl necklace would have. She very smoothly, without hesitation, removed a long pearl handled knife from a scabbard that was strapped around her thigh. She smiled, sat back down and placed it on the table in from of her.

There was a free and careless devil-may-care demeanour about this beautiful woman. And, as Fernando glanced down at the glimmering blade of the weapon, with a sort of sinister joy, he was surprised at how she was making this whole affair a visual delight. It was obvious she was out of money and ready to use that weapon as a tool to barter for a loan.

"How much do you think that's worth?" asked Smothers.

"Don't know," replied Deanna. "Those are genuine South Pacific pearls and the blade is tempered steel."

He tried the point, then he snapped it under his thumb nail and a little shiver of a ringing sound reached as far as where Fernando was sitting. Then Deanna suddenly leaned a little across the table, pointing toward the hand in which Smothers held the pack of cards, ready for the deal.

Smothers shook his head and gripped the pack more closely. "Do you suspect me of crooked dealing?" he asked as he pushed back his chair and stared intently at her.

Very coolly, with no emotion evident, Deanna said, "I think you'll keep that hand and that same pack of cards on the table until I've had it looked over. I've dropped a thousand to you, and you're winning it with stacked decks."

Smothers had been confronted before and always come out best, but he had never been confronted by a woman. He had no respect for this woman, looking at her as he would a stray cat on the sidewalk. He said, "You're mighty bold for a little lady with a fancy knife."

"Before you can whip out that derringer you are concealing under your sleeve, I'll have this knife with the blade pointed directly at you buried in your heart," said a deadly serious Deanna.

The derringer would not be brought out because Deanna was swift and sure. This was no ordinary woman he was facing. She struck as a grizzly strikes when it claws the fish out of the stream. She struck as fast as the snap of the bullwhip. And well and truly did that steel find its home, not in the real heart, but in the heart of a gambling man. The heart for Smothers was his dealing hand. The dull, chopping sound of the blow stood by itself for an instant. Then Smothers, looking down in horror at his hand, with the blade of the knife buried between his index and forefinger, screamed and fell back in his chair.

THE GIRL WHO RODE INTO A STORM

That was the instant when Fernando judged his lieutenant and found him wanting. A man who fainted in such a crisis as this was beyond the pale. Other people crowded around the fallen Smothers. Frightened and desperate, Fernando pushed his way to his lieutenant. At length his weight enabled him to squeeze through the rapidly gathering crowd of gamblers. The only nonchalant person of the lot was she who had actually used the weapon. For Deanna stood with her shoulders flexed backward as she now raised the dress on the opposite side, revealing another gorgeous leg that carried a death dealer. She had a small calibre gun strapped to that leg. She whipped it out faster than a rabbit jumping out of a briar patch. A certain calm insolence about her expression reminded Conner, who stared in amazement at what was transpiring, of his friend Dudley, as Deanna said to the gathering throng of onlookers, "The fiery dragon can spit fire in a lot of ways, be careful anybody who thinks I don't mean business. I sure do hate to bust up a nice little party like this one has been, but I figure those cards are stacked. I have a pile of reasons for knowing, and I want somebody to look over the cards, a neutral party, but somebody that knows stacked cards when he sees them. Mostly it isn't hard to get onto the order of them being run up. I'll leave it, gents, to the man that runs this dump," as she, leaning across the table, pushed the pack straight to Fernando. The latter gritted his teeth. It was very cunningly done to trap him. If he said the cards were straight they might be examined afterward; and, if he were discovered in a lie, it would mean more than the loss of Smothers; it would mean the ruin of his business. Did he dare take the chance? Must he give up Smothers? The work of years of careful preparation had been squandered on Smothers.

Fernando looked up, and his eyes rested on the calm face of Deanna Defoe. Why had he never met someone like her before? There was a real winner! There was a woman with steel-cold nerve, worth a thousand trained men like Smothers! Then he glanced at the wounded man, cowering and bunched in his chair. At that moment the gambler made up his mind to play the game in the big way and pocket his losses.

"Ladies and gentlemen," he said sadly, as he gently tapped Smothers on the shoulder indicating he should go along with him, "I am sorry to say that this brave little lady is right. The pack has been run up. There it is for any of you to examine" he said, pointing to the cards on the table. "I don't pretend to understand. Most of you know that Smothers has been with me for years. Needless to say, he will be with me no more." And, turning on his heel, the old fellow walked slowly away, his hands clasped behind him, his head bowed.

As people are prone to do, they fall in line to follow those who play them like a fined tuned Stradivarius. The crowd poured after him to shake his hand and tell him of their unshakable confidence in his honesty. This was the way of a world where people were like sheep. They mindlessly followed their manipulators off a cliff to fall into the abyss of misery. Conner placed his right hand on Deana's shoulder and as she turned around there was a familiarity to her gaze that rocked his soul. Those eyes were the window to a world where love that could not be consummated dwelled. He knew that she was unattainable. He could see it in her eyes, but he could also see just how much she loved him. It was all there right in front of him. He was committed to another woman, and Deanna knew it he sensed, but she had an emptiness in her, because she could not be with Conner for some reason. He could see a hurt deep within her soul.

Deanna said to Jerry Jones, as she pointed at the drawer under the table, "There it is. Take it."

"How much do I take?"

"All of it," she said. Then she pointed at the other gentleman who had played. Give these theirs back, and the rest is ours. Nobody is going to argue with you."

"But there are thousands there."

"Take it. The house loses, its all ours and nobody will stop us from walking out with it," she said as she looked over at a seated Fernando across the room who knew he could do nothing.

The diffident Jerry fingered the money in the drawer of the table. Deanna said, as he swept it up and thrust it into his pockets, "Split it later. Dudley is waiting. He knew I could expose this charade, and he will be pleased."

THE GIRL WHO RODE INTO A STORM

In the entry hall, as they made their way toward the door, they found Fernando in the act of dissuading several of his clients from leaving. The incident of the evening was regrettable, most regrettable, but such things would happen when wild men appeared. Besides, the fault had been that of Smothers he pleaded. He assured them that Smothers would never again be employed in his house. He had discarded all care for the wounded man. Secretly, of course, he would hand him a bundle of money and arrange for him to take up residence with a gambling house he had in Santa Fe.

Fernando turned to the three and said, "I apologize for what has occurred here."

Deanna said, "You need a word with these gents and a man named Dudley Danforth. I'll send him over in a few minutes." He is awaiting me outside down the street. She then turned to her companions and said, "Go with this man, and Dudley will join you soon. Don't be afraid of him," she said as she looked at Fernando, "because if he harms you, I'll come back and cut his heart out."

As she started to leave, she motioned for Conner to come to her by the door. Conner noticed as her succulent lips parted and she began to speak a flaw that he had not noticed before. It was almost comforting to see that even a beautiful woman like Deanna could have a least one minor flaw. She had a slightly chipped left incisor tooth that in no way detracted from her beauty.

THE GIRL WHO RODE INTO A STORM

She whispered to him. "You make a future with Carmine Jones. You have no future with me my darling man, because there is something about me that prevents me from ever being your wife. I shall always treasure the times we were together. Although ever so brief, they have filled my heart with the kind of love I never dreamed possible. Thank you for that."

She turned and left as Conner stared in disbelief that a woman such as she could have any feelings for him, but he knew that this would be the last time he would ever see her. With a heavy heart, he turned back to the two men, and Fernando motioned for them to follow him as he told a compatriot to watch for Dudley and bring him to his office. Conner and Jerry went to Fernando's office, a little apartment which opened off the main entry to the casino. It was furnished with an almost feminine delicacy of style, with wide-seated, spindle-legged Louis XV chairs and a couch covered with rich brocade. The desk was French provincial. A small tapestry with embroidered gargoyles made a ragged glow off the wall behind Fernando's desk.

Dudley was shown in by a stern looking fellow. He greeted Fernando with a nod, as Fernando said, "You are aware that I could have placed your friends here in the hands of the police for what they have done. I mean, regardless of what happened they have stolen money from me."

"My friend," said Dudley while Fernando was flushing with anger at his nonchalant attitude, "police might have grabbed them, but they would have grabbed your casino as well. A reputation for being a cheat is not good for business."

"That is true," said Fernando hotly, "this will be your last visit here, and I may pay a big price for letting you walk away."

"In all probability it will indeed be our last visit. Remember that we are letting this drop and walking out with money they would have won anyway if the game had been on the up and up."

"The incident is closed," Fernando said with gravity, and he leaned forward, as if to rise.

"Keep your seat" said Dudley to Fernando as he looked over at the stern fellow by the door "and tell that fellow by the door that if I see him move for his gun, the first person I am shooting is you, and you'll be dead before his bullet hits me. There are a few questions you have to answer, and then we may or may not be on our way. It is our call, not yours."

Fernando stayed seated and palpable fear was obvious as Dudley said, "I have an idea that you worked the whole deal. This is a square house, Fernando, I could tell that right away. Why were we three and then our beautiful compatriot picked out for the dirty work?"

It required all of Fernando's long habits of self control to keep him from going into a rage. He managed to look into Dudley's eyes, and he could see this was a man who meant business. He eased back into his chair to show that he was not challenging him.

THE GIRL WHO RODE INTO A STORM

Dudley said, "Suppose I get down to cases and name names? The gentleman, and I use the term loosely, who talked to you about us was John Markham. Am I right?"

"Sir," said Fernando, thinking that his world was about to crumble before his eyes, "what…"

"I'm right," said Dudley. "I can tell when I am by the way a person's face wrinkles up. I sure hurt you that time, Fernando. John Markham it was, then."

Fernando could merely stare as Dudley was now answering his own questions as his two compatriots sat silently and observed this superb tactician at work. "Out with it," said Dudley.

Fernando bit his lip in thought. He was by no means a coward, and three alternatives presented themselves to him. One was to say nothing and pretend absolute ignorance; the other was to drop his hand into his coat pocket and fire the little automatic which nestled there, or to order his bodyguard by the door to open fire, but the later two scenarios seemed likely to lead to his own death.

"Listen," said Dudley, "suppose I was to go a little farther in my guesses. Suppose I said I figured out that John Markham and his men might be scattered around outside this casino, waiting for me and my two friends here to come out. What would you say to that?"

"Nothing," said Fernando, but he blinked as he spoke. "For a feat of imagination as great as that I have only a silent admiration. But, if you have

J. WAYNE FRYE

some insane idea that John Markham, a gentleman I know and respect greatly, is lurking like an assassin outside the doors of my casino, you are sadly mistaken."

"Or maybe his men have worked themselves inside the casino and are lurking about right now."

"If you think that," replied Fernando, "I can only keep silent. But, to ease your own mind, I'll show you a simple way out of the house, a perfectly safe way which even you cannot doubt will lead you out unharmed. Does that bring you what you want?"

"That sounds," retorted Dudley, "like a credible way for us to leave this place. Lead the way, and you'll find us right at your heels." Then Dudley pointed at the bodyguard and continued, "And he stays here."

"No problem," said Fernando as he got up and led the three down towards the cellar. They paused at last in a cool, big room and the unmistakable scent of the underground was in the air.

"Here we are," said Fernando, as he picked up a lantern, lit it and illuminated the room while drawing aside a curtain which opened into a black cavity.

Dudley approached and peered into it. "How does it look to you, Jerry?" he asked.

"Dark, but good enough for me, if you're all set on leaving this way. You've not been wrong up to this point, so I have placed myself in your capable hands. Any man who can come up with a woman like Deanna is a man I trust."

THE GIRL WHO RODE INTO A STORM

"I don't care how it looks," said Dudley thoughtfully, "but looks can be deceiving. For example, our friend Fernando here probably looked at Deanna and thought how beautiful she was and so very feminine, but he never dreamed how deadly she could be. However, with me there are ways of smelling things, and the smell of this tunnel isn't good to me. Look again and try to pry down that tunnel with that lantern Fernando is holding."

Accordingly, Jerry snatched the lantern from Fernando and held it level with his head. They saw a tunnel opening, with raw dirt walls and a floor and a rude framing of heavy timbers to support the roof. But it turned an angle and went out of view in a few feet.

"Go down there with your lantern and look for the exit," said Dudley as he stared at Fernando.

The damp cellar air seemed to affect the throat of Fernando as he coughed heavily.

"Say, Dudley," said Jones, "looks to me that you're carrying this caution too far. Let's take a chance on what we've got ahead of us?"

Fernando was chuckling: "You show a touching amount of trust in me, Jerry."

Dudley turned on him with an ugly sneer. "I don't like you, Fernando," he said. "There is nothing about you that looks good to me. If I knew half as much as I guess about you I'd blow your head off, and go on without ever thinking about you again. But I don't know. Here you've got me up against it. We're going to go down that tunnel;

but, if it is a trap, Fernando, it will be the worst day of your life."

"Take this passage, or I'll take you back up and escort you out the front door. Do you want starlight and John Markham or a little stretch of darkness, all by yourself?" asked Fernando.

Dudley studied the face of Fernando, almost wistfully. The more he knew about the fellow the more thoroughly convinced he was that Fernando was bad in all possible ways. He might be telling the truth now, however, or he might be simply tempting him on to a danger. There was only one way to decide. Dudley was, like Deanna, a gambler, so he mentally flipped a coin and nodded to Jerry.

"We'll go in," he said, "but I am not feeling good about this."

They walked into the damp air of the tunnel, reached the corner, and there the passage turned and ended in a blank wall of raw dirt, with a little apron of fallen debris at the bottom of it. Dudley walked first, and, when he saw the passage obstructed in this manner, he whirled like a flash and fired at the mouth of the tunnel. A snarl and a curse told him that he had at least come close to his target, but he was too late. A great door was sliding rapidly across the backside of the tunnel, and before he could fire a second time, the tunnel door closed. Jerry Jones ran at the door, which had and struck the whole weight of his body against it. There was not so much as a quiver. The face of it was hardened steel.

THE GIRL WHO RODE INTO A STORM

Dudley sat down, as he spoke, cross-legged, and the last thing Jerry saw, as he snapped out the light, was the lean, intense face and the blazing eyes of Dudley. In the meantime the light was out, and the darkness sat heavily beside and about them, with the faint succession of inaudible breathing sounds which were sensed rather than actually heard.

"Suppose we had some dynamite," said Dudley cheerily.

"Sure, but we haven't," said Jerry."

"We might be able to find some," said Dudley.

Jerry Jones groaned. "Are you trying to make a joke out of this?"

"No joke. You think Fernando is joking?"

"Fernando ain't going to leave us in here. Nope, he's going to find a way to get us out. That's easy to figure out. But the way he'll get us out will be as dead people, and then he can dump us, when he feels like it, in the river," said Conner.

"Then the thing for us to do is to get set and wait for them to make an attack? No use waiting. When they attack it will be in a way that will give us no chance," offered Dudley.

Conner interjected a note of hopelessness when he said, "Then we are lost."

"Unless we can get out before they make the attack. There may be something behind the dirt wall at the end of the tunnel."

"Nonsense," said Jerry.

"There is something behind that pile of dirt I'm telling you," said Dudley.

J. WAYNE FRYE

Conner stood, and said, "Then lets check it out."

The other two obediently went down to pass the turn and come again to the ragged wall of earth which terminated the passage. Jerry held the lantern and passed it close to the dirt. All was solid.

"Hold on a minute," whispered Dudley. I saw something." He snatched the lantern, and together they peered at the patch from which the dried earth had fallen.

"Queer for hard clay to break up like that," muttered Dudley, cutting into the surface beneath the patch with the point of his knife. Instantly there was the sharp gritting of steel against steel. It was very clear. They had dug the tunnel to this point and excavated a place which they had guarded with another steel door, but, in order to conceal the hiding place, or whatever it might be, they cunningly worked the false wall of dirt against the face of it, using clay and a thin coating of plaster as a base.

"It's a place they don't use very often, obviously," said Dudley, "and that's why they can afford to put up this fake wall of plaster and mud after every time they come down here. It is pretty clever to leave that little pile of dirt on the floor, just like it had been worked off by the picks. All we have to do is to get to the door and into whatever lies beyond."

"We'd better hurry, then," said Jerry.

"What's the rush?" pleaded Conner.

"Take a breath," said Dudley.

THE GIRL WHO RODE INTO A STORM

All three men inhaled deeply and the air was beginning to fill rapidly with the pungent and unmistakable odour of burning wood! No great intelligence was needed to understand the meaning of it. Fernando, having trapped his game, was now about to kill it. He could suffocate the three with smoke, blown into the tunnel, or make them rush blindly out. The moment they appeared, dazed and uncertain, the revolvers of half a dozen gunmen would be emptied into them.

They had only to turn the corner of the tunnel to be sure. Fernando had the door of the tunnel slid noiselessly open, then, into the tunnel itself, smoking, slowly burning, pungent pieces of pine wood had been thrown, having been first soaked in oil. The tunnel was rapidly filling with smoke, and through the white drifts of it they looked into the lighted cellar beyond. They would run out at last, gasping for breath and blinded by the smoke, to be shot down in a perfect light.

Dudley said, "Quick, dig. We have to find that door behind the dirt."

Jerry had already turned. In a moment they were back and tearing with their fingers at the sham wall, kicking loose fragments with their feet. All the time, while they cleared a larger and larger space, they searched feverishly with the lantern for some sign of a knob that would open the steel door, or some button or spring which might be used to open it. But there was nothing, and in the meantime the smoke was drifting back, in more and more unendurable clouds.

J. WAYNE FRYE

A voice called from the mouth of the tunnel, and they could recognize the smooth tongue of Fernando. "I think I have you now. But trust yourselves to me, and all may still be well with you. Throw out your weapons, and then walk out."

"I'll die in here blazing my gun in your direction, first," said Dudley, as they continued to dig at the dirt. The surface of the steel was still covered, after they had cleared it as much as they could, with a thin, clinging coat of plaster which might well conceal the button or device for opening the door. Every moment the task became infinitely harder.

Finally Jerry, his lungs nearly empty of oxygen, cast himself down on the floor and gasped. A horrible gagging sound betrayed his efforts for breath. Dudley and Conner knelt beside him, their own lungs were burning. They were all on the verge of exhaustion and separately sucking for air.

"Come on men, come on, one more try," pleaded Dudley, "then we'll turn and rush them and die fighting."

The others nodded in agreement and stood. Together they made that last effort, fumbling with their hands across the rough surface, and suddenly they touched the spring area and a section of the surface before them swayed slowly in.

Dudley pushed his two compatriots through the opening and they tumbled into a small room and fell to the floor exhausted. Dudley staggered after. They gasped for air like new born babies, as someone behind them closed the steel door.

THE GIRL WHO RODE INTO A STORM

They began to breathe easier and then there stood the person who had closed the door – Rena Tilson. While they sucked in air, all they could do was stare with shock at her.

.

Chapter 10
Freedom for You is Non-Negotiable

Presently Jones and Conner sat up, and Dudley's head cleared rapidly as he stared at Rena. They found themselves in a small room, not more than ten feet square, with a ceiling so low that they could barely stand erect. As for the furnishings and the arrangement, it was more like the inside of a safe than anything else. There were three small stools in a corner and a series of steel drawers and strong chests, lining the walls of the room and leaving in the center very little area in which one might move about. Rena, in an evening cloak, was grabbing Dudley by the arm and leaning a pale white face close to him. "Hurry!" she was pleading. "There isn't a minute to lose. They will find out, guess where you are and then…"

"John Markham?" asked Dudley.

"Yes," she exclaimed, realizing that she had said too much, and she pressed her hand over her mouth, looking at the three in a sort of horror.

Jones and Conner had come to their feet at last, but remained in the background, staring with befuddled minds at Rena. Dudley gazed at her, with a strange blending of pity and admiration. He knew that the danger was not over.

"This way!" pleaded Rena as she led them toward an opposite door, very low in the wall.

Dudley said, "You don't have to rush. They won't start going through the smoke for awhile. They'll think they've choked us, when we don't come out shooting. But they'll wait awhile to make sure. We have time to learn a lot of things that we'll never find out, unless we know right now, pronto!"

He stepped before Rena, as he spoke. "How did you know we were in there? How did you get down here? Why would you risk everything to let us out through this obvious treasure laden vault of a room?"

Rena, really pleading now said, "Do you mean you want to stay here and talk? Even if you have a moment to spare you must use it. If you knew the men with whom you are dealing you would never dream of tarrying here."

Dudley, grimacing with determination, said, "Rena, I've seen square things done in my life, but I've never yet seen a girl throw up all she had to do a good turn for a man she's seen only once."

"You're a fool," she replied.

Smiling, Dudley said, "My guess is that you're one of John Markham's best cards. He uses you on the big game."

She had drawn back, one hand pressed against her breast, her mouth tight with the pain. "You have guessed all that about me?" she asked faintly. "That means you deplore me!"

"What folks do doesn't matter so much," said Dudley. "It's the reasons they have for doing things that really counts, and the way they do it. I don't know how John Markham made a tool out of you, but I do know that he hasn't changed the goodness in you."

Dudley was never particularly forward with girls. Now he acted as gracefully as if he had been Rena's father. "Rena," he said, "to your credit, you've saved three lives tonight. We've got to go, but I'm not forgetting this."

"You must go yes, and you must never see me or Carmine Jones again, not even you, her brother," she said as she looked over at Jerry Jones, "should ever see your dear sister again. Leave Denver, all of you. Leave it as quickly as you can, and never come back. Only hope that his reach isn't long enough to follow you."

"Leave?" Dudley asked. "I'll tell you what you're going to do, Rena. When you get back home you're going to tell Carmine that Jerry, here, has seen the light about Markham, and that he has money enough to pay back what he owes."

"But I haven't," said Jerry. "Part of it is yours"

THE GIRL WHO RODE INTO A STORM

"It is all yours," said Dudley, "Yours so you and Carmine can get out of this desperate life you are living and hopefully she will go with my friend Conner here and make a new life for herself and him."

Jerry bowed his head as Dudley continued. "Rena, let Carmine know that there are no chains on anybody, and, if she wants to find Conner, all she has to do is go across the street, walk away from that evil house where Markham rules with an iron fist. You understand?"

"But, even if I were to tell her, how could she go, when she's watched constantly?"

"If she can't get to a man like Conner, here, who is waiting for her, right across the street, she isn't worth having," said Dudley sternly.

"I'll tell her," she said as she hurried before them leading them through the door, and then conducted them down a passageway. It was deadly black and silent, but the rustling of Rena's dress, as she hurried before them, was their guide. And always her whisper came back: "Hurry! Hurry! I fear it is too late!"

Suddenly they were climbing up a narrow flight of steps. They stood under the starlight in a back yard, with houses about them on all sides. "Go down that alley, and you will be on the street," she said.

"We'll go, and we'll wait for Carmine and you, too!"

"Don't talk madness! Why will you stay? You risk everything for yourselves!"

J. WAYNE FRYE

Jerry Jones was tugging at Dudley's arm to draw him away, but he was stubbornly pressing back to Rena. He had her hand and would not let it go. "If you don't show up Rena to free yourself of this evil man," he said, "I'll come to find you. You hear?"

"Bless you, but never venture here again," she said as her hand slipped from his, and she was gone into the shadows.

Back at the gaming house, Fernando sat at his usual table fuming over the fact his prey had escaped him. Rena walked in the front door as if nothing had happened. However, there was more trouble at Fernando's table. John Markham was sitting with him, with his back to the room. To see Fernando was bad enough, but to see the master mind of all the evil that passed around her was disheartening. She tried to ease by him and move to the bar, but Markham said, as she passed, "Just a minute, Rena."

For a moment there was a frantic impulse in her to bolt like a foolish child afraid of the dark. After an imperceptible hesitation, she turned.

She went to him and found that he was leisurely and openly examining her, his chin resting on one hand, his thin face perfectly calm, his eyes hazy with contempt. It was a habit of his to regard her like a picture, but she had never become used to it; she was always disconcerted by it, as she was at this moment with her blood pumping rapidly. He rose, when she was beside him, and asked her to sit down, which, of course, she did.

"But I've hardly flirted with a single man," she said. "This isn't very professional, you know, wasting a whole evening."

His voice was firm. "Sit down."

She obeyed, positively inert with fear, sitting across from him. He said, "Do you think I keep you at this detestable business, because I want the money?" he asked. "Rena, is that what you think of me? I have wanted to make you a free and independent being, my dear, and that is why I have put you through the most dangerous and exacting school in the world - the school of hard knocks. You understand?"

"I think I do, yes," she replied falteringly.

"But not entirely do you. Go back to the old days, when you knew nothing of the world but me. Can you remember?"

"Yes, yes!"

"Then you certainly recall a time when, if I had simply given directions, you would have been mine. I could have married you the moment you became a woman. Is that true?"

"Yes," she whispered, "that is perfectly true."

"But I didn't, at the time, want a whore for a wife." You would have been a very undeveloped child, really; you would never have grown up. No matter what they say, something about a woman is cut off at the root when she marries. Certainly, if she had not been free before, she is a slave if she marries a man with a strong will. And I have a strong will, Rena, very strong! So you see I faced a problem if I married you before you were wise enough to know me. You would have become a slave, shrinking from me, yielding to me, incapable of loving me. No, I wanted a free and independent creature as my wife. I wanted a partnership you see to put you into the real world, and let you see it for what it is? I could not do that in the ordinary way. I have had to show you the hard and bad side of life, because I am a hard and bad man myself."

His face was fierce; his eyes were wistful, entreating her not to agree with him, but such a sudden rush of pity for the man swept over her that she put out her hand on his. He looked down at her hand for a moment, and she felt his fingers trembling under that gentle pressure.

"I understand more now," she said slowly, "than I have ever understood before. But I'll never understand entirely."

"A thing that's understood entirely is despised," he said, with a careless sweep of his hand. "A thing that is understood is not feared. Even love is nothing without a seasoning of fear. For instance, I am afraid of you, dear girl. Do you know what I have done with the money you've made over the years?"

"No."

"I have contributed half of it to charity."

"Charity!" she exclaimed.

"And the other half," he went on, "I deposited in a bank to the credit of a fictitious person. That fictitious person is, in flesh and blood, Rena Tilson with a new name. You understand? I have only to hand you the bank book with the list of deposits, and you can step out of this life and appear in a new part of the world as another being. Do you see what it means? If, at the last, you find you cannot marry me, my dear, you are provided for. Not out of my charity, which would be bitter to you, but out of your own earnings. And, lest you should be horrified at the thought of living on your earnings as a whore, I have thrown bread on the waters. For every dollar you have in the bank you have given another to charity, and therefore, your horrible profession has helped others maybe avoid that profession."

She, almost in whisper, said, "Then I am free? Free, John?"

"Whenever you wish."

"Not that I ever shall wish, but to know that I am not chained, that is the wonderful thing." She looked directly at him again: "I never dreamed there was so much fineness in you, John Markham. I never dreamed it, but I should have!"

"Now I have been teaching Carmine to the game," he went on, "and she is beginning to love it. In another year, or six months, trust me to have completely filled her with the fever. But now enters the mischief-maker in the piece, a stranger, an ignorant outsider. This incredible man named Dudley arrives and, in a few days, having miraculously run Carmine to earth, goes on and brings her face to face with that man Conner, teaches Jerry Jones that I am his worst enemy, steals enough money from Fernando to pay off his debt to me, and convinces Jerry I can never use my knowledge of his crime to jail him, because I don't dare bring the legitimate authorities too close to my own rather explosive record."

"I saw them both here" said Rena, wondering just how much Markham really knew, "and I also saw that beautiful woman Deanna who is, no doubt, their confederate."

She saw his keen eyes probe her with a glance. But her ingenuousness, if it did not disarm him, at least dulled the edge of his suspicions.

Sombrely, Markham said, "Dudley was here, and the trap was laid for him, and he slipped through it. Got away through a certain room which Fernando would give a million to keep secret. At any rate, the fellow has shown that he is slippery and has a sting, too, not to mention that beautiful Deanna who is more deadly than a rattle snake in the desert sun at high noon."

"I am sorry that you are having so much trouble, John."

Smiling, he said, "Really sorry, uh? Well, there is something you can do about it. What I want is to secure Carmine from the inside. I want you to go to her, to persuade her to go away with you on a trip. Take her out west, any place you please. The moment this guy Conner thinks his lady is running away from him of her own volition he'll throw up his hands and curse his luck and go home. Will you go back tonight, right now, and persuade Carmine to go with you? Will you do that for a man who has done so much for you?"

THE GIRL WHO RODE INTO A STORM

She bowed her head under the shock of it. Dudley had begged her to send Carmine to meet Conner. She was torn between the freedom Markham was dangling before her with all that money, and the reality that she would be condemning Carmine to a life in service to Markham. She sighed and said, "Do you think she'd listen?"

"Yes, tell her that the one thing that will save the head of Conner McCord is for her to go away, otherwise I'll kill the fool. Better still, tell her that Conner of his own free will has left Denver and given up the chase. Tell her you want to console her with a very nice trip. She'll be sad and glad and flattered, all in the same moment, and go along with you without a word. Will you try, Rena?"

"I suppose you are earnest when you say that you would kill Conner McCord if he continued to be a nuisance?"

"No doubt about that. Will you do your best?"

She rose very deliberately. "Yes," she said. "I'll go back to the house right now."

Smiling, he said as he looked over at Fernando, who had intently sat silently through the entire conservation, "Thank goodness that I have one person in whom I can trust without question, one who needs no bribing or rewards, but works to please me. Good-by, my dear."

He watched her leave the casino, and then got up, looked down at Fernando and said, "Foolish girl," as he signalled for Miles Morgan to come over from a nearby table. Miles scurried over obediently. "Shadow her," said Markham.

"On it boss."

"She'll probably talk with Carmine. Find a way of listening. If you hear anything that seems wrong to you, anything about Carmine leaving the house alone, for instance, telephone to me at once. Now go. I am depending on you."

Rena left the gaming house entirely convinced that she must do as John Markham had told her. It was not until she had climbed to Carmine's room and opened the door that her determination faltered. For there she saw the girl lying on her bed weeping. And it seemed to the poor, bewildered brain of Rena Tilson that though Markham had ordered the girl to be confined to her room until further notice, no one in the house would think of questioning Rena, if she took the girl downstairs to the street and told her to go on her way. She closed the door softly and, going to the bed, touched the shoulder of Carmine. The poor girl sat up slowly and turned a stained and swollen face to Rena.

Through tears, Carmine said, "He's changed his mind? He's sent you to tell me that he's changed his mind, Rena? Oh, you've persuaded him to it. I know you have!"

Rena walked to the bathroom, moistened the end of a towel, returned and began to remove the traces of tears from Carmine's face. That face was no longer flushed, but growing more radiant with excitement and hope.

"It's true?" she kept asking. "It is true, right, Rena?"

"Do you love him as much as that?"

"That I cannot say for sure, but I love the idea of being free of this life. When I went to Minnesota to be with that horrible manager of the correspondence school, who bought me for a few months from John, I wrote to Conner as a fluke, and then when I was preparing to return I ask him to meet the train on the way through Dry Gulch. I was only guessing about him, and when he didn't meet me, I felt all was lost and that there was no way out of here. I went cold and made up my mind that I would never think of him again."

"But when you saw him in the street, here?"

"I was angry with him, and brainwashed by John. But, when Dudley Danforth talked to me that night, I knew that Dudley cared very deeply for this man, too. So deeply that he would risk his life to see his friend happy with me."

"Yes," whispered Rena, nodding and smiling faintly. "I remember how he stood there and talked to you. He was like a man on fire to help his friend."

"Yes, I have never seen anyone so devoted to a friend."

Rena sighed. "Yes, it borders almost on the obsessive his devotion to Conner. I can understand your attraction to Conner, because I feel he is also just as devoted to Dudley. Seeing two men with that much concern for one another makes you know that they would also exhibit that concern for wives as well. Still," she said with a broad smile, "in our line of work, you know, one has to study character, and that Dudley is a different sort."

"Very different," agreed Carmine.

Then a great inspiration suddenly came to Carmine. Rena was a key to escaping this terror. "Do you know what we are going to do?" she asked gravely, rising.

"What?"

"We're going to open that door together, and we're going down the stairs."

"Together? No, Carmine. John is not a man to trifle with. He has ordered you to stay here."

"They won't dare stop us if you are with me, leading the way."

"Carmine, are you mad?"

"It is obvious you have strong feelings for Dudley," said a determined Carmine. "We both have a chance now. Come with me and see just how far we can get from this horrible life we live in this despicable place."

She took Rena by the arms and turned her until the light struck into her eyes. Rena, aghast at this sudden strength in one who had always been a meek follower, obeyed without resistance. Was she going to defy Markham? Was she going to forgo money for hope? She felt herself driven irresistibly forward to face a future free of the restraints imposed by an evil man. It suddenly occurred to her that Markham was playing her for a fool, manipulating her just as he had always done. What he told her at Fernando's was a lie.

Still, she hesitated. "Carmine, I am not in love with Dudley. He is an adorable man, but there is something that tells me he is not capable of genuinely loving me. This is foolish for me."

"Then go to him not as I am going to Conner, with my heart in my hands, but to ask Dudley to take you away somewhere, so that you can begin a new life."

"Ask charity of a stranger?"

"You know he isn't a stranger, and you know it isn't charity. He'll be happy. He's the kind that's happy when he is helping someone."

"Yes," answered Rena, "of course he is. But you don't understand. John, John has…"

"And don't you trust Dudley?"

"To the end of the world, but to leave…"

"Rena, you don't see what's happening to you. John Markham hypnotizes you. He makes you think that the whole world is bad, that we are simply making capital out of our crimes. As a matter of fact, the cold truth is that he has made me a thief and a whore, and he has made you the same."

Carmine began to pull Rena slowly to the door. Still, Rena was protesting. She could not throw herself on the kindness of Dudley. But the door opened, and she allowed herself to be led out into the hall. They had not made more than half a dozen steps down its dim length when the guard hurried toward them.

The guard hurriedly came up to them. "Sorry," he said. "Got an idea you're headed downstairs,

Carmine. Can't allow that until the boss gives his approval. And I got to ask you to step back into your room, and step quickly. Please don't make my job difficult."

Carmine was ready to start back, and as she was on the verge of turning, the arm of Rena passed strongly around her shoulders and stayed her. "She's going with me," she told the guard. "Does that make a difference to you?"

"Sure it makes a difference. You go where you want, any time you want, but this lady ain't going no place but her room."

"I say she's going with me, and I'm responsible for her."

She pushed Carmine forward, and the latter made a step, only to find that she was directly confronted by the guard, who said, "I got my orders."

"They're old orders," insisted Rena, "and they have been changed. Walk on, Carmine. If he blocks your way I'll call John and this cretin will be on the streets where he belongs."

"Go on then you two. You'll regret this!"

They hardly heard the last of these words, as they turned down the stairway, hurrying, but not fast enough to excite the suspicion of the man behind them.

They reached the floor of the lower hall, and a strange thought came to Rena. She had hurried home to execute the bidding of John Markham. She had now defied him only partly as a result of Carmine's forcefulness. The real reason was that dandy dude named Dudley who was as strange a character as she had ever met. Yet, there was something about him that touched her and also mystified her.

They scurried to the front door. As they opened it the sharp gust of night air blew in on them, and they heard the sound of a man running up the steps. In a moment the dim hall light showed on the slender form and the pale face of John Markham was staring at them.

Carmine felt the surprise of Rena. For her part she was on the verge of collapse, but a strong pressure from the hand of her companion told her that she had an ally in the time of need.

"My, oh my" Markham was saying, "What's this? How did Carmine get out of her room, and with you of all people, Rena?"

"It's idiotic to keep her locked up there all day and all night, in weather like this. When I talked to her this evening I made up my mind that I'd take her out for a walk."

"Well," replied John Markham to the two frightened ladies, "that might not be so bad. Let's step inside and talk it over for a moment."

They retreated, and he entered and locked the door behind him. "The main question is where do you intend to walk?"

"Just in the street below the house," replied Rena.

"Which might lead you across to the house on the other side?"

"Certainly not! I shall be with her."

"But suppose both of you go into that house, and I lose the both of you instead of just one? I would be devastated. What of that my clever little Rena, with the deceptive look?"

She knew at once by something in his voice, rather than his words that he had managed to decipher what went on in Carmine's room. She asked bluntly: "What are you guessing at?"

"I am guessing at nothing. I only speak of what I know. No single pair of ears is enough for a busy man. I have to hire help, and I get it. Very effective help, too, don't you agree?"

"Eavesdropping!" exclaimed an angry Rena. "You sent me to steal her from her lover, and I've tried to steal her for him in the end. Do you know why? Because she was able to show me what a happy love might mean to a woman. She showed me that, and she showed me how much courage love had given her. So I began to guess a good many things, and, among the rest, I came to the conclusion that I had rather have my honour than that money you claim to have for me."

He turned from her and faced Carmine, and, though he smiled at her, there was a quality in the smile that shrivelled her very soul with fear. Rena said to him, "I want to take Carmine with me to freedom and the man she loves. Surely you have somewhere in that hard heart of yours some compassion for people who are in love. You cannot be totally callous and without any feeling whatsoever for two people who are young and seek some happiness with each other."

THE GIRL WHO RODE INTO A STORM

The lean fingers of John Markham brushed though his thick hair. "Only that?" he asked. "My dear, how strange you women really are. After all these years of study, I should have thought that you would, at least, have partially comprehended me. I see that is not to be. But try to understand that I divide with a nice distinction the affairs of extreme sentiment and the affairs of business. There is only one element in my world of sentiment and it is always overridden by economic considerations. This is America my dear, the land where money talks and anything else can walk. I have money invested in both of you, and tonight, I had nearly nine thousand dollars taken by a woman of steel who was assisted by Conner McCord, Jerry Jones and that prancing fancy dandy, Dudley Danforth. Now, I am going to discount that as the cost of doing business with dishonourable people, but why on earth should I let Carmine here walk away? You were made for this life Carmine, and dear Rena, you are an entirely different matter. Can you comprehend it? Is it clear? As for giving you freedom Rena, you will never have it as long as I have breath. Freedom for you is non-negotiable!"

Chapter 11
Let's Go

The assuredness of John Markham's comments made the two women sink into despair. Rena stood stoically as Carmine began to sob and sunk into a chair.

"Help me, please, Rena," she implored pitifully. "No other person in the world can help me but you!"

"Do you see how she needs to be free of this life," asked Rena quietly of John Markham, "and still it doesn't move you?"

"Not at all."

"Suppose I take my own freedom, and I tell the police that in this house a girl is being held against her will."

"I own most policemen. You should know that."

THE GIRL WHO RODE INTO A STORM

"I warn you that all your holds on her are broken. She knows her brother has the money to pay you now. She knows that Dudley has broken her chains, Jerry's chains, all of our chains."

"Dudley Danforth may seem to have the upper hand, but those old holds I have are not equal to the new ones I will acquire. If you leave now, I can even promise you my dear that before the next day dawns, the very soul of Carmine will be a pawn in my hands. Do you doubt it? Such an exquisitely tender, such a delicate soul as Carmine. Can you doubt that I can form invisible bonds which will hold her even when she is far away from me?"

"Suppose," Rena said, "I were to offer to stay?"

"You tempt me, with such overwhelming generosity to become even more generous myself and set her free at once. But, alas, I am essentially a practical man. If you will stay with me uncontested, why then I will make this girl as free as the wind. You see, I must have you by fair means or foul, but I cannot put any chain upon you except your own word. I confess it before this poor girl, if she is capable of understanding, which I doubt. Do you truly stand by your offer?"

She hesitated, and then he went on: "Be careful. I have had you once, and I have lost you, it seems. If I have you again there is no power in you, no power between earth and heaven to take you from me a second time. Give yourself to me with a word, and I shall make you mine forever. Then Carmine shall go free."

Rena looked to him, she looked to Carmine. The latter had suddenly raised her head and threw out her hands, with an unutterable appeal in her eyes. At that mute appeal Rena surrendered.

"It will be done, because I know there is something in Dudley that would keep him from accepting me. What could I do in the world out there except what you've taught me to do? No, let Carmine go, and I will stay willingly here with you."

Rena crossed the room slowly and stood before him. "I am yours now and forever."

"You are free to go," said John Markham to Carmine.

"Rena," whispered Carmine.

Rena turned away, and the movement brought Carmine beside her, with a cry of pain. "Don't make this sacrifice for me."

"Carmine!" broke in John Markham.

She turned at the command of that familiar voice, as if she had been struck with a whip. He had raised the curtain of the front window beside the door and was pointing up and across the street. "I see the window of that man's room," he said. "A light has just appeared in it. I suppose he is waiting. But, if you wish to go, your time is short; my offer is for only a short time."

An infinite threat was behind the calmness of the voice. She could only say to Rena with tears in her eyes: "I'll never forget this." Then she fled into the foyer, out the door and the two within heard only the sharp patter of her heels on the street.

THE GIRL WHO RODE INTO A STORM

It was freedom for Carmine now, and Rena, lifting her eyes, looked into the face of the man she was now stuck with. A vague astonishment came to clear her mind. There would be no joy in the future.

Markham took her arm forcibly, and they went slowly up the stairs, and at each landing it seemed her strength gave out, and she had to pause for a brief rest. He whispered to her, "This pain will not last. You'll learn to, as you did before, love serving my needs, love obeying my every command."

She said nothing, only forlornly bowed her head in complete supplication to he who had ruled her life for so long that she had forgotten what freedom was like.

He, in a very low voice, said, "You remember the old Greek fable, Rena, the story about all the pains and torments which flew out of Pandora's Box. I know that sending that girl over there without you will open a Pandora's Box. That is why I did it, not to give her freedom, but to give myself freedom – the freedom to kill those men who dared to think they could best me. I cannot let this go. It simply is not in my nature. I cannot be bested by that strutting peacock of what isn't even, in my eyes, a man. He is an abomination."

"You promised. You promised." screamed Rena.

He opened the door to her bedroom, shoved her in hard, closed it and said through the door that he bolted from the outside. "The next sounds you hear will be of gunshots. The days of those

J. WAYNE FRYE

meddling miscreants are about to come to an end. I am turning this place into a fortress protected by 12 hard men, because I know Dudley Danforth will not allow you to stay here. He is a fool who believes in honour of the highest order, and he will not let this lie anymore than I will."

Rena felt more alone than at any other time in her life. Raising her head she found she was looking straight across the street to the lighted windows of the rooms of Dudley and Conner. She imagined the silhouettes of a man and woman running to each other, seeing them clasped in each other's warm arms. Rena suddenly dropped to her knees and buried her face in her hands, sobbing like a baby.

Meanwhile, Markham had his well-armed crew station themselves strategically to repel what he knew would be an assault on the home to free Rena. He began to feel exhilarated as he gathered up his Winchester slide action repeating rifle, sat down in the library at the top of the stairs and contemplated how he would get pleasure out of seeing that prancing peacock of a man Dudley beg for his life. He hoped he would not be killed right away by his men, because he wanted the chance to stand over him and give him the coup de grace.

Once Carmine was out in the street she had cast one glance of terror over her shoulder at the towering facade of the Markham's house, then she fled, as fast as her feet would carry her, straight across the street and up the stoop steps of the rooming house and frantically up the stairs.

She was tapping hurriedly and loudly on a door, while, with her head turned, she watched for the coming of some swift-avenging figure from behind. She knew in her heart that it was impossible for John Markham to give up anything he owned, and he felt he owned Carmine. When would he strike? That was the overriding question in her mind.

Then the door opened. The very light that poured out into the dim hall was like the reach of a friendly hand, and there was Dudley smiling while Conner stared in disbelief.

"I told you, Conner, and here she is," said Dudley. Yet, his joy was a bit subdued as he watched the two embrace in a long lingering hug. He sighed deeply and sat down in a chair by the window.

"How did it come about that he let you leave," asked Conner.

"He just did it. I believe he is afraid deep in his heart of Dudley."

Staring at the frowning face of Dudley, her heart for a moment palpitated with regret. How could she tell the truth? How could she admit her cowardice which had accepted Rena's great sacrifice?

"I need some questions answered," said Dudley.

"Won't they wait?" asked Carmine.

"No, they cannot wait. What made Markham change his mind about you?" he asked. "He isn't the sort to change his mind without a pretty good reason."

THE GIRL WHO RODE INTO A STORM

Carmine hung her head in shame, but could not find the words to tell him what happened, as Dudley said, "What bought him off? Nothing but a high price would change a man like that, and you are here alone. I think I know what the price was."

And she had to admit: "It was Rena. She was the price."

"She made a promise to stay so that you could go free?" said Conner.

"Rena was preparing to come with you?" asked Dudley.

"Yes."

"And when Markham stopped you, she offered herself in exchange for your freedom?"

"Yes."

Both she and Conner looked apprehensively at the dark face of Dudley, where a storm was gathering. But he restrained his anger with a mighty effort as he said, "She was going to cut away from that life and start over."

"Yes."

"Get the police, Dudley," said Conner. "They sure can't hold no woman agin' her will in this country."

"In this country Conner, those with money can do anything they want. That is the way it is, and probably always will be. Anyway, it is her will to be there. Don't you think she's ready and willing to live up to it? She went to the limit for the three of us."

Conner, with knowing eyes, looked at Dudley and said, "You ain't letting it lie are you?"

"He knows I am not the kind of person to let something like this lie. That is why she is over here. He is gunning for us in that house where he is holding Rena."

Conner, put his hand on his holstered gun and said, "You been through hell for me. Here's where I go as far as you go. I'm ready when you're ready"

It was so righteous an offer from Conner that Carmine dared not cry out against it, but she sat with her hands clasped close together, her eyes begging Dudley to let the offer go. Conner looked at her. Then he forlornly said, "Do you love that woman?"

"I can't love any woman Conner. I can't explain it, but it just isn't there. This is not about love. This is about honour." Then, he looked over at Carmine and said, "We put your brother on the train, and gave him half the money we took, nearly 4500 hundred dollars. We saw no need to pay off Markham, because he has been cheating all of you for years. Under that bed is the other 4500 dollars. If we don't make it back, you use it to set yourself up in business, and make sure, if we get Rena out, she is your partner."

She could not find any words; all she did was rise and hug Conner, because she knew his devotion to Dudley precluded any hope of pleading with him not to go. After that long hug, Conner turned to Dudley, took out his revolver to make sure it was loaded with six bullets, placed it back in the holster and said, "Let's go."

Chapter 12
I'll Never Have That

Like a symphony beginning with a low, sombre, soft melody, the two reluctant gunfighters walked nonchalantly, but with determination out of the apartment into the hallway. There, two children were playing jacks on the landing. They looked up at the men and smiled. Dudley tipped his hat and Conner smiled back at them. It was as everything was in slow motion. The two men appeared totally unafraid, shoulders back, heads unbowed. The sound of their boots on the stairs were like cymbals clanging as the symphony builds to a crescendo.

At the bottom of the stairs, Dudley looked over at Conner, smiled and said, "It's been a pleasure to be by your side."

Conner returned the smile as he replied, "Likewise, friend."

Dudley pushed open the door and side by side they walked down the stoop steps into the blackness of a street of dreary loneliness that wrapped them in its shadowy, melancholy, caliginous arms as if to say, "welcome to the dark." It was so dark that even the shadows of the two were not reflected on the street or the walls of buildings around them. The stars and the moon seemed to be cowering in dread as they hid behind a dense layer of cloud cover, giving the air that tincture associated with a coming storm. The senses of the two men were becoming more acute now, as they started the slow walk to the building across the street where evil awaited in a house that was not a home, because it welcomed the pain of empty souls. In that dark place there was no compassion, no remorse as the dark side had been embraced by all save one - Rena. There was pleasure in cruelty there and the only joy was in the use of power to dispense evil.

The lights were on in the house across the street, but they were as dim as a shrouded ghost wrapped in the haze of a dying dream. The house seemed to be pulsating with the hopelessness of a yawning grave waiting for an occupant.

Conner said, "Do we go in blazing?"

Dudley replied, "We go in quietly through the alley. We'll crawl through the same basement window I used the first time there. The place will be filled with his henchmen, waiting to dispatch us as quickly as possible. I know the house, so let me lead."

Just as they were stealthily moving toward the side of the house, the front door sprang open and out popped two men with guns drawn. Dudley and Conner dropped to the street as bullets whizzed over their heads. "I got the one on the left," shouted Dudley, as his gun spit lead into the heart of the assailant while Conner's shot split the skull of the other one, brains splattering against the front door. They sprang up in an instance and bolted for the door, tossing aside any hope of surprise by entering from the rear of that dark, gloomy house of despair. Rapidly firing, they leaped over the dead men on the stoop and bounded through the doorway. Lying on the floor, they rolled over on their backs and reloaded their guns as they heard movement at the top of the stairs. A shadow of a tall man with a rifle in his hands could be seen at the first stair landing. Conner and Dudley both fired at the same time and the man tumbled head first down the stairs.

Suddenly, to their left and right, two men bounded out of the darkness with six-shooters blazing. One of them slightly grazed Conner in the left arm with one of his three shots, but Conner's aim was far better and the man took a load of lead in his stomach, dropping his gun as he desperately tried to keep his guts in with both hands. He wasn't successful.

Dudley rolled on his side and shot the other assailant under the chin, the bullet ricocheting up through his jaw into his head and spilling brain matter as he tumbled forward, falling on top of Dudley, who suddenly realized that dead men are heavier than broken hearts. He pushed him off as he and Conner got up and cautiously moved toward the stairs.

At that point, four of the men tossed their rifles down the stairs and shouted, "We're through. Don't shoot."

Dudley said, "Move slowly toward the top of the stairs, hands up. As they got to the landing, Dudley motioned them down the stairs. He whispered to one of the men, "How many left up there?"

"Four including the boss," was the reply.

"Get out of here," whispered Dudley, and the men scurried down the stairs like jack rabbits in boots, nearly falling as they ran for the front door.

Dudley called out, "It is stupid to die for a man who is finished. It's over for Markham. Toss your weapons out and walk away. Your comrades were smart."

The darkness down the hallway that led to Rena's room offered minimal cover, and the top of the landing was obscured as it turned to the left. Dudley and Conner were on the top stair, and were scared of moving onto the landing for fear of exposure.

The iciness of intense reality was slowly overwhelming them. It was an act of foolishness they may have embraced. It might well be an epoch of folly and incredulity. Yet, within

THE GIRL WHO RODE INTO A STORM

Dudley and Conner's hearts, there was the spring of hope as they stood there together. Across the plains of time they had forged a bond far beyond friendship.

An eerie silence reigned over the house now. There was desolation, lifelessness. There was no movement. The air was thick with death and decay so alone and cold that the spirit of it was like a banquet of lost tranquility. There was a hint in the house of laughter, but of laughter more terrible than any sadness, a contrived laughter that was as mirthless as the smile of the Sphinx in the vast Egyptian desert. It was the masterful and incommunicable wisdom of eternity laughing at the futility of life and the effort it took to get through it. Thus was this place where misery of the spirit had come to dwell, and its chief practitioner was John Markham, and in this den of torment, desolation and distress he had imprisoned Rena in a web of evil.

No live organism can continue for long to exist sanely under conditions of absolute control. This evil house lacked a soul and stood by itself against compassion as within its walls beat the heart of evil. The floors were firm and silent in a detestable homage to wretchedness, and the doors were insensitively shut against any moral light. The evil silence lay steadily against the wood and stone of this monstrous house, and what walked there whispered of corrupt, villainess wickedness.

THE GIRL WHO RODE INTO A STORM

It is said that God created man and that Samuel Colt made them all equal. Maybe Samuel Colt was more reliable than God, because God obviously made a mistake when he created John Markham. On the other hand, Samuel Colt turned out a perfect instrument to do the job for which it was intended, killing. Still, despite Conner and Dudley both carrying Colt 45's, they were not equal to the three men hiding in the dark hallway, because they were more familiar with the surroundings than the two brave men at the top of the stairs waiting to rescue Rena.

The silence was becoming foreboding now. Dudley motioned for Conner to pick up one of the rifles dropped on the top stair by the men who had decided to give up the fight. He signalled for him to fling it out in the hallway for a distraction, and when the men in the hallway opened fire, they would bound around corner of the landing with guns blazing in the direction where they would pick up the flash of the guns going off.

A mighty heave sent the rifle flying down the hallway and all three men opened fire in the direction of the rifle, as Dudley and Conner lurched into the hallway and aimed precisely at the places where the firing was coming from. The firing from them stopped abruptly with the sound of bodies falling to the floor.

As Dudley started for Rena's room, the door to his left opened, and there stood Markham. He took a deep breath and said, "You fancy peacock of a man, I'll have to hand it to you. You have bested me, but you will not leave here alive. With that brief statement, he charged Dudley who told Conner not to shoot. Markham threw his big left fist toward Dudley's right jaw. Dudley ducked under it and gave him a stiff right hand to the solar plexus, knocking the wind out of him. He then reached down between his legs and with an astute bit of leverage lifted him up off the ground onto his back. Markham grunted, and went limp as he lay unconscious on the floor. The little guy had bested the big guy and stood staring down at Markham as he said to Conner, "get Rena and let's get out of here before we have to explain this carnage to the police."

Rena came running to Dudley and threw her arms around him. There did not have to be words, because her gratefulness showed in her eyes. Rena peered down at Markham who was regaining consciousness. He looked up at her and extended his right hand and from beneath his sleeve a derringer flipped out, and he fired its single shot into Rena's breast. She crumbled into Dudley's arms as Conner unloaded every shot left in his gun into Markham's body.

Rena looked at Dudley as she gasped for breath. Her last words were, "You are the finest man I have ever known."

Dudley gently lay her down on the floor, looked up at Conner and through tears said, "And she was the finest woman I ever knew. She gave her life for a friend."

I am sorry, but we have to go," said Conner.

Now actually crying, Dudley, looking deeply into Conner's eyes said, "You have something to go to. I will never have that."

Epilogue
Into the Storm Unafraid

Getting out of Denver was a breeze for Dudley, Conner and Carmine. Their timing was perfect for boarding the train to Boulder even before the police had showed up at Markham's home to survey the carnage. Once in Boulder, the three bought horses and rode to the little town of Longmont. Saddened by the loss of Rena, who had made it possible for Carmine to escape, they arranged anonymously for her burial. Dudley was instrumental in working out a deal for Carmine and Conner to purchase a restaurant with the money they had taken from Fernando and Markham. The three rode together to look at a ranch that might make a perfect place for Carmine and Conner to call home.

THE GIRL WHO RODE INTO A STORM

Thick, dark, foreboding storm clouds were forming on the horizon. It was as if the weather was signalling a coming calamity, or perhaps it was just a revelation of reverential testaments flowing down from the heavens to assure them that the end of one tyranny, the worst being hypocrisy, can foretell the beginning of another. After all, America was a nation of tyrannies against so many people who were always on the outside looking in. For most Americans, there was no hope or no justice as the few had turned the nation into a monopolistic playground for the rich and well-connected. Or, perhaps the weather was nothing more than a customary storm for that time of the year. The clouds oozed and billowed across the now disappearing sun. A jagged bolt of lightning ripped the sky in half, and afterward the thunder rolled precipitously across the terrain seeming to crack the earth like a tortured chord of harmony from an ill-playing band. A violent wind suddenly ripped Carmine's hair around her face, and Dudley's long pony tail fluttered in the breeze. They did not flee the coming storm in fear, but merely galloped with more intensity.

Conner looked at Dudley and said, "You know what? This storm reminds me of Deanna Defoe. In her own way, she was a raging storm of contradictions. She was actually stronger than any man I have ever known, including you."

Carmine, feeling a tinge of jealousy, for she knew that Conner had strong feelings for Deanna, said, "Her contradictions are because she is like the soft breeze on a warm evening. She blows in for only a brief time and then disappears into anonymity. There is something strange about her, something that prevents her from a normal life that all we women desire."

Dudley said, "Normality eludes many my dear Carmine. For some of us, normalcy is but a dream that can never be fulfilled because of barriers erected through no fault of our own, barriers erected by a society that had rather condemn than accept, barriers by a society that abstains from the knowledge offered by scientists who study human beings and the mental and physical properties that make us who we are, and, above all, by religion that preaches more hate than love. Religion is the one single element that one day I sincerely believe will destroy this country. Religion turns every argument and disagreement into an us versus them paradox. Religion doesn't allow for dialogue or open communication. Everything is either black or white with no shades of grey. Righteousness, according to the pontificating buffoons who prance about in the pulpits spewing hate make goodness a product of self, not Jesus. And when righteousness is a product of self, everyone must think like you. It breeds pride and arrogance. This is why religion causes wars, and causes people to always be condemning rather than showing compassion and understanding. The more someone disagrees with a person's religion, the more offended and upset they become. Eventually, the anger and pride imprison those who cannot nor will not understand the folly of their own self-contradictions."

Conner took a deep breath and reflected on Dudley and how he looked different from other men, but that was his choice, as he chose to dress the way he did in defiance of the norm, and, being the strong minded man he was, Dudley would never bow to convention.

Conner looked over at Dudley, noticing that his bedroll was awfully thick. He curiously ask him, "Why the big bedroll, Dudley?"

"I'm heading back to Montana, my friend. I've packed all my belongings."

"Why? We got a good thing going here," offered Conner.

Carmine said, "Yes, we are a family Dudley. We need you with us."

"Carmine, I will never have a family. That is not my destiny, but yes, you and Conner are the closest I will ever come to having a family." He looked over at Conner and continued, "One day Conner and Carmine, you will understand me and my way, but I am not sure you are ready for that right now."

They came to the crossroads where there was one road straight ahead back to Longmont, and the other to their left that led to Billings. Dudley pulled back on his reins. "This is where I leave you."

"We wish you would not go," said Carmine, and Conner simply could find no words, as he fought back tears.

THE GIRL WHO RODE INTO A STORM

Dudley smiled at Conner, and Conner noticed he had a slightly chipped incisor. Dudley turned his horse, looked back over his right shoulder and said, "Goodbye," as he galloped off.

Conner was crying now, as he looked at Carmine and said, "You know who that is?

"What do you mean? It is our friend Dudley."

"No, he is not really Dudley. Carmine my dear that is Deanna Defoe (same initials as Dudley Danforth), the real woman I love, but she is not a woman as you and I know one. She is a woman who lives in hell trapped in the body of a man. There is a new fangled phrase for what Deanna has. It is called gender dysphoria. I am sorry, but I cannot let her go. You are a wonderful woman, but I must be by Deanna's side. She needs me and I need her."

"Tears filled Carmine's eyes as she said "Go then my love. Go, because I love you both, and I know you will have to fight the prejudice of a world with no heart and no compassion, but go, please go, hurry and catch her, and never leave her side."

Conner smiled at her with the deepest affection imaginable. This was true love she was showing him. He pulled back his reins and pointed his horse in the direction taken by Deanna, and galloped off in pursuit of the person he truly loved as the storm was building in intensity. The raging tempest was in front of him now. The clouds were darkening and the wind was swirling about. Rain was starting to fall as Conner galloped up beside the person he loved. He looked over, stared with intensity and said as he looked at the turbulent disturbance ahead. "We'll be in a storm the rest of our lives, but I do not care as long as I have you by my side." He reached over and took her soft hand and said, "We ride into this together unafraid because our love will be our sword and shield."

Deanna stuck out her chest proudly, smiled and still with her hand held tightly by Conner, galloped off into the storm unafraid.

The End

Wayne Frye's books are known for their surprise endings and for their profound pontificating on the human condition. If you enjoyed this book about a transgender person, do not miss his books about transgender private eye Chablis Louise Chavez from Peninsula Publishing and Fireside Books

Chablis: Avenging Angel for the Forgotten
In the City of Lost Hope
Chablis and the Terrorist
The Disappearance
Pursuit
Chablis and the Dildo from Hell
Chablis and Lynton in the Room of Doom

THE GIRL WHO RODE INTO A STORM

Also Available from
Fireside Books
By J. Wayne Frye:

The Lynton Adventures

Lynton Curls Her Hair
Lynton Walks on Water
Lynton and the Vampire at Tagaytay Manor
Lynton Buys a New Cell-Phone and Hears the Voice of Doom
Lynton Viñas and Beowulf Perez in the Taal Inferno
Lynton and the Ghosts in the Mansion on Balete Drive
Lynton Viñas: Shadow in the Darkness
Lynton's South African Adventure
Lynton, the Karoo Vampire and the Jewels of Omar Bin Abi
Lynton and the Stellenbosch Terror
Pursuit (Adult)
Chablis and Lynton in the Room of Doom (Adult)

The Aaron Adams Hardboiled Detective Series

When Jesus Came to Canada to Lead an Indigenous Rebellion
White Meteors and the Ghost of Sue Ann McGee
Hockey Mania and the Mystery of Nancy Running Elk
Something Evil in the Darkness at Hopkins House
The Girl Who Motivated Murder Most Foul
The Girl Who Stirred up the Whirlwind
The Girl Who Said Goodbye for the Last Time
When Jesus Came to Jersey as the Son of Thunder
Fall From Apocalypse
Armageddon Now

Non-Fiction

How Hockey Saved a Jew From the Holocaust
Worth Part 1: Roaring Through Life Like a Comet in the Midnight Sky
Worth Part 2: The Night of Thunder Road
Canadian Angels of Mercy – Nurses in Times of Peril
Points of Rebellion: Aboriginals Who Fought for Justice

J. WAYNE FRYE